She hadn't planned to go this far…

But she didn't want to bring the night to a close. For the first time she wasn't thinking about the future, about the inn. This night belonged solely to them—to her—and she wasn't ready for it to end.

Paul cleared his throat. "Maybe I should go."

"Why?"

"I think you know why."

She told herself he'd ask her out again and maybe they'd finish what they'd started. Or maybe they could just finish it now, she thought, nibbling his lips. She felt a quiver run through him.

"I'm a big girl, Paul. I haven't had a vacation in three years. I have a rare few hours for myself, and a very handsome, occasionally charming man with whom to spend them. Now, I could light a candle and we could play gin rummy, or we could adjourn to my bedroom with no strings and no regrets."

His smile flashed in the dim light. "Well, when you put it that way…"

* * *

Bride Mountain:

Wh… r away…

A PROPOSAL AT THE WEDDING

BY
GINA WILKINS

Published in Great Britain 2014
by Mills & Boon, an imprint of Harlequin (UK) Limited,
Eton House, 18-24 Paradise Road, Richmond, Surrey, TW9 1SR

ISBN: 978 0 263 91271 5

23-0314

Harlequin (UK) Limited's policy is to use papers that are natural, renewable and recyclable products and made from wood grown in sustainable forests. The logging and manufacturing processes conform to the legal environmental regulations of the country of origin.

Printed and bound in Spain
by Blackprint CPI, Barcelona

Gina Wilkins is a bestselling and award-winning author who has written more than seventy novels for Mills & Boon. She credits her successful career in romance to her long, happy marriage and her three "extraordinary" children.

A lifelong resident of central Arkansas, Ms. Wilkins sold her first book to Mills & Boon in 1987 and has been writing full-time since. She has appeared on the Waldenbooks, B. Dalton and *USA TODAY* bestseller lists. She is a three-time recipient of a Maggie Award for Excellence, sponsored by Georgia Romance Writers, and has won several awards from the reviewers of *RT Book Reviews*.

For my writing friends,
who commiserate the dark days, celebrate
the good days, and are always there with
encouragement and the occasional crack of the whip.

Chapter One

The farmers' market bustled with shoppers on this warm Tuesday morning in early July. Bonnie Carmichael browsed the outdoor displays of fresh fruits, vegetables and herbs, occasionally making purchases and adding the bounty to the increasingly heavy canvas bags dangling from her arms. She should have brought her little wheeled market trolley, she thought with a shake of her head. She'd told herself that not having it with her would make her less likely to purchase too much, but instead she was simply juggling bulging bags.

She loved visiting the farmers' market, surrounded by the bright colors of fresh produce, cut flowers, handcrafted pottery and jewelry, the scents of fresh-baked bread and pastries, the sounds of chattering shoppers and busking musicians. The market was even more active on Saturdays, but it was hard for her to get away on weekends from the bed-and-breakfast she co-owned and operated with her two older siblings. She was the chef at the inn, so shopping was both her responsibility and her pleasure. She came to the market regularly enough that most of the vendors knew her by name.

She was chatting with a local organic farmer, lifting a plump heirloom tomato for an appreciative sniff, when someone bumped hard against her arm, having been jostled by someone else in the milling crowd. The tomato fell to her feet with a squishy thump.

"I'm so sorry," a man said immediately, his voice coming from approximately a foot above her head. "Are you okay?"

She looked up to assure him no harm was done, but felt the words freeze on her tongue when she recognized Paul Drennan.

This just couldn't be happening again.

Twice, Bonnie had run into Paul—literally—at the inn in the Virginia Blue Ridge Highlands. The first time she'd met him, in May, she'd carried a box of stainless steel wine bottle stoppers that had scattered around her when she'd landed on the floor. He'd been with his twenty-one-year-old daughter, Cassie, who was planning an August wedding on the grounds of the inn, and Bonnie had been mortified to crash into a client. The second incident a few weeks later had been his fault; he'd been talking over his shoulder while walking and had barreled into her, though she'd managed not to fall that time.

It should have come as no surprise that the next time she encountered him, only a couple of weeks later, it would be with another collision. Or that once again she was as jarred by her immediate and powerful attraction to him as by the physical contact. Something about this man had taken her breath away the first time she'd looked up at him from the floor where she'd landed. She'd felt a spark between them when he'd offered his hand to help her to her feet, a clichéd reaction she hadn't expected, but had seemed very real, all the same. Apparently, nothing had changed. Her pulse tripped again in response to seeing him here.

Beneath a thick shock of dark auburn hair touched with a few white strands at the temples, Paul's jade-green eyes lit with a smile that meandered more slowly to his firm lips, drawing her attention there. "If this keeps happening, you're going to file a protection order against me," he said in the deep voice she remembered so well from those other two brief meetings. She'd heard it a few times in her daydreams since, she thought sheepishly. "I swear I'm not actually targeting you."

"I believe you," she assured him with a weak laugh. "It is getting rather funny, though, isn't it?"

Using a paper towel given to him by the vendor, he quickly cleaned up the half-smashed tomato. "I'll pay for that one," he promised the good-natured farmer, who waved off the offer.

Handing some bills to the vendor, Bonnie accepted a bag of pretty little multicolored heirloom tomatoes in exchange. When she fumbled a bit with the new bag, Paul reached out to help. "Let me carry a couple of those sacks."

He divested her of all but the smallest of the bulging bags before she could even respond. As he did, she smiled up at him—way up. She estimated him to be perhaps six feet three inches, in marked contrast to her own five feet three inches. The flat sandals she wore with her scoop neck mint top and summer print skirt gave her no extra height. “Thank you.”

“You’re welcome. How’s business at Bride Mountain Inn?” Paul asked as he shuffled with her through the throng to the next booth.

“The past few weeks have been hectic with June weddings,” she replied. “And July hasn’t slowed down much.” Trying to focus on her reason for being here, rather than the man who’d unexpectedly become her shopping assistant, she examined a crookneck squash in a display basket.

“Being busy with weddings is a good thing, right?”

“Absolutely.” Though she’d already bought so much, she couldn’t resist picking out a few squash.

“Those look good,” Paul said, nodding toward her selections. “I like squash, but I don’t know how to prepare them.”

“Oh, they’re easy to cook,” she assured him. Her momentary self-consciousness dissipated with this subject she could discuss comfortably. “Very versatile, baked, grilled, steamed or even raw in salads.”

She didn’t know if Paul had any interest at all in cooking, but he nodded attentively. “I like them all those ways. Just haven’t tried cooking them myself. Do you have time to help me select a few? I’ll look up some recipes online.”

“Of course.” Speaking briskly and casually, as she would with just anyone who’d asked for her help, rather than a man who happened to make her toes curl in her sandals, she gave him a quick lesson on checking the stems, skin and heft-weight for ripeness and freshness.

She watched as he paid for four then stuffed them into his own market bag. A price tag still hung from one strap, making her suspect he'd purchased it when he'd arrived. It appeared to be almost empty.

Seeing the direction of her attention, he chuckled. "I guess you can tell I'm new at this sort of shopping. My daughter has been lecturing me lately about eating better, so I figured this was as good a place as any to buy a few healthy ingredients. I usually just throw bags of frozen vegetables in the microwave to eat with whatever meat I've cooked on the grill. Or I have takeout. But Cassie's staying with me for the next few weeks until her wedding, so I'm trying to be a little more health-conscious when it's my turn to cook."

"You sound like my brother. If I didn't cook dinner for him fairly often, he'd live on spaghetti with sauce from a jar, or grilled steaks and microwaved potatoes."

Paul's crooked smile was undeniably charming. "I've eaten more than my share of both those meals."

Someone cleared her throat rather loudly, making Bonnie aware that she was blocking access to the squash. She'd completely lost track of where she was and what she'd been doing while she'd admired Paul's smile. Murmuring a quick apology, she moved aside, followed again by Paul.

He motioned toward a little coffee shop near the market where several outdoor tables beneath colorful umbrellas invited a leisurely chat. "May I buy you a cup of coffee? Or do you have to rush back to the inn?"

She hesitated before answering. He'd given her the perfect excuse, but she really wasn't in a hurry to get back. Rhoda and Sandy, her full-time and part-time housekeepers, were taking care of things back at the inn. Even during this busy season, Tuesdays were typically slower-paced days, giving Bonnie a weekly opportunity to escape for a few hours.

While there were advantages to living in the inn's private basement apartment, it gave her the feeling sometimes of being at work 24/7. She'd made a promise to herself recently that she'd start going out more, cultivating a social life away from the inn and her siblings, out of the rut she'd fallen into during the past few years. A friendly coffee with one of the inn's clients wasn't exactly a groundbreaking departure from the norm, but it was a start. It didn't hurt, of course, that this particular client was so very nice to look at across a table.

"I don't have to rush back," she said. "Coffee sounds good. Just let me put these bags in my car."

He followed her to the parking lot where she'd left her dependable sedan and helped her stash her purchases. Then she accompanied him to the coffee shop, claiming a recently vacated outdoor table while he went inside to order. He returned carrying a black coffee for himself and the fat-free iced latte she'd requested in deference to the building heat of the day. She'd declined his offer of a snack, but he'd bought a cookie for himself.

"It's oatmeal raisin," he said with an appealingly sheepish grin as he unwrapped it. "That's healthy, right?"

Because there didn't seem to be an ounce of fat on his solid frame—something she had noticed more than once—she doubted his diet was as bad as he'd claimed earlier. "Sure," she teased lightly. "Keep telling yourself that."

He chuckled and took a big bite of the cookie, washing it down with a sip of his coffee. "I'll make up for it at dinner tonight," he said. "I'm eating with my daughter's other family. Holly—my daughter's mom—always cooks something fancy and healthy."

Bonnie had briefly met Cassie's mother, Holly Bauer, and her husband, Larry, at that first pre-wedding meeting back in May. As she remembered, the relationship between them all had been quite cordial.

"It's nice that you and your ex-wife get along so well," she commented somewhat tentatively. "We've dealt with some very awkward situations at a couple of weddings at the inn when exes refused to be seated near each other or to even acknowledge the other parent's presence."

"Holly and I were never married," Paul admitted. "I was only eighteen and Holly not even quite that when Cassie was born—she'd skipped a grade to graduate a year earlier than most. We were the stereotypical high school sweethearts who slipped up on prom night, I'm afraid. We stopped trying to be a couple during our freshman year of college, though we've remained good friends."

"I see." She'd figured Paul looked young for his age, considering he had a twenty-one-year-old daughter, but now she knew he really was younger than she'd thought. Thirty-nine? Only eleven years older than her twenty-eight, rather than the fifteen years or more she'd estimated. "And still Holly became an attorney. Good for her."

"Yeah. She refused to let one night's bad decision derail her dreams. She had a lot of help from her family, and from me, and from my mother during the first two years of Cassie's life, but Holly worked her butt off to finish her education and still be a good mom. She earned her undergraduate degree in three years, then entered law school. A law school friend introduced her to Larry, and they married when Cassie was almost six. Their twins were born a year after that."

"Holly sounds amazing. It's nice that you've stayed friendly for Cassie's sake."

"It's been for my sake, too," he assured her. What might have been wistfulness momentarily clouded his eyes when he explained, "I lost both my parents fairly young. Holly and Larry have been generous enough to include me in their family so that I was able to be a big part of Cassie's life—and of the twins', for that matter. They call me Uncle Paul. They've spent almost as many weekends with me as Cassie has.

"Larry's a really great guy," he added quickly, "but he's a brainy engineer who has no interest in sports or outdoor activities, so I was the one who taught Cassie and the twins how to throw a ball and cast a line and ride a horse. I guess some people would consider it an odd arrangement, but it's worked very well for us."

Bonnie thought it was rather charming, though she couldn't help wondering how other women in Paul's life felt about him remaining so close to his daughter's mother. She could see how it might be intimidating for an outsider to try to make a place for herself in that cozy arrangement. Was there a woman in Paul's life now? She could think of no subtle way to ask.

She really had been too narrowly focused on the inn for the past few years, she thought ruefully. It would be three years in October since she and her brother and sister had inherited the place from their late, maternal great-uncle, and the first of November would mark their second anniversary of reopening to guests after a year of renovations. Those three years had been busy and challenging, leaving little time for a social life. She'd almost forgotten how to flirt, and she could hardly remember the last time she'd gone beyond flirtation. It was definitely time to address that situation. She had even considered signing up with an online dating service.

She supposed she could consider this impromptu coffee break as practice…or maybe a possible beginning? Paul had certainly remained in her thoughts after their previous meetings.

"It sounds as though Cassie and her siblings had a close extended support system," she said, trying to stay focused on the conversation. "That had to be good for them."

Paul nodded, his expression suddenly hard to read. "Yeah. It's been great. But a lot of things are changing. For Cassie and for me."

With a slight shake of his head, he reached again for his cookie before she could decide how to respond. "I don't usually tell my life story over coffee, but since you'll be helping us with the wedding arrangements, I figured you'd want to know you don't have to go out of your way to accommodate the bride's parents. Nor do you have to worry about anything unpleasant occurring during the event. We're cool with whatever works best for Cassie and the wedding planner."

Bonnie chuckled. "That is very helpful. But I have little to do with the actual wedding ceremony. My sister handles the arrangements with the planner and the subcontractors. I take care of the inn itself—hosting overnight guests, preparing and serving breakfast six days a week, Sunday brunch and a light supper Sunday evening, and any special food orders not handled by an outside caterer. Our brother takes care of the grounds. He'll hang special lights or put up torches or garland or whatever else Cassie wants for decorations."

"You have your responsibilities well-defined."

"When you're dealing with siblings, that's the best plan of action," she said, knowing Logan and Kinley, her brother and sister, would heartily agree.

He laughed. "I can imagine."

Kinley and Logan had been a bit hesitant about the massive undertaking of refurbishing and reopening a 1930s-era inn that had been closed to guests for eighteen years before it had been willed to them, especially considering the state of the economy at the time. Great-uncle Leo Finley had done his best to keep the place up but it had become too much for him to do more than basic maintenance. After he'd lost his dear wife, Helen, who had been his longtime partner in both life and business, he hadn't had the heart to keep their inn running. But neither had he been able to sell the establishment his own father had built and operated for years. Leo's will had bequeathed the inn and a sizable life insurance policy equally to his great nieces and nephew, with full permission for them to do with it as they wished—though he'd known it was Bonnie's lifelong dream to reopen it.

Bonnie had begged and cajoled her brother and sister into investing everything they had—financially, emotionally, physically—into restoring their heritage. Or as her sister termed it, she had "bullied" them into it. Bonnie knew her petite blonde appearance could be deceptive. She might look like a pushover, but when she set her mind on something, she could be tenacious.

With her degree and experience in hotel management, Kinley's marketing and sales background, and Logan's computer training and eclectic interests in landscaping and construction, she had assured her siblings they had a fighting chance for success. What was the worst that could happen? she'd asked. Bankruptcy? A hard pill to swallow, but they could recover from that eventually, as long as they had each other.

Maybe that final argument had been a little cheesy, but it had worked.

"We're pleased that Cassie chose the inn as the venue for her wedding," she said sincerely. "I promise we'll all do our best to make the experience everything she hopes for."

"I'm sure you will. Cassie said she had a good feeling about the inn the first time she saw it."

"I'm glad. She seems like a sweetheart."

Obviously, she'd found Paul's weakness. His jade eyes warmed as his smile softened. "I'm biased, of course, but I think she's pretty special. Smart as a whip, like her mom. She graduated as her high school's valedictorian, will complete her bachelor's degree with honors in August, and is already accepted into an elite graduate program in London starting in January. She's studying fashion design. She's very talented."

There was something especially appealing about a man who was so unabashedly crazy about his child. "Family man" was number one on the list of qualities she would look for in a potential partner. She'd always thought she would like to marry and perhaps start a family someday, but before she committed fully to anyone, she would have to be very sure he was completely ready to settle down, prepared to work as hard as she at making the union last. The total opposite of her own footloose father, who'd left his family when Bonnie was only four to pursue his own ever-restless dreams of traveling the world.

"I can tell you're very proud of Cassie. With good reason, obviously."

He grimaced good-naturedly. "I know, I'm bragging shamelessly. I'm having a hard time accepting that she's about to marry and move to another continent. I tried to talk her into waiting a couple of years, but she and Mike are determined to get married now, so I've just had to accept her decision. Still, it seems like just last week I was tucking her into bed after letting her eat a forbidden fast-food burger and ice cream sundae for dinner."

"Did you let the twins have forbidden food, too?"

He winked at her. "Why do you think they consider me their favorite uncle?"

Bonnie was enjoying this conversation. Having spent so much time lately with her reticent, taciturn older brother, it was nice to chat with a man who was comfortably talkative. "Good conversationalist" was high on that list of desirable traits in a man, followed by "good sense of humor."

"Speaking of food..." She glanced down at the market bag at his feet, wondering if what she was about to suggest was foolish. "I don't know if you're interested or have time, but beginning next Tuesday, I'm teaching a few classes in cooking with seasonal produce. The classes will meet at the inn for the next three Tuesday evenings from six until eight and we'll cover buying produce, knife skills, cooking methods and ways to preserve fresh produce for off-season use."

Her sister had told her that Paul taught high school, which probably explained why he was free today on a summer weekday. Maybe he was looking for something else to do during his break?

His eyebrows rose, though she couldn't quite tell if it was from surprise, interest or both. "You're teaching cooking classes?"

She nodded. "I was sort of pressured into it by a woman who has booked several social events at the inn. She thought it would be fun if she and a few of her friends took cooking lessons, and she asked if I would consider teaching them at the inn. I have room for six in the class, but one dropped out so I have an opening."

"I didn't know you offered classes."

"I have on occasion, usually during the off-season—Kinley's idea to keep people coming into the inn even when we have few outdoor events scheduled. I've conducted several one-day specialty classes like cupcake decorating, or making jams, jellies and preserves, or candy-making. This will be my first multisession class. I understand, of course, if you're not interested, but you mentioned you'd like to learn to cook fresh produce..."

"Actually, I would be interested. I just happen to have the next three Tuesday evenings free, and it would be great to spend them learning how to do something useful. Cassie would definitely approve."

She was rather surprised by how quickly he'd jumped on her offer. She'd thought at the most, he would agree to consider it. Was he really that excited to learn to cook—or maybe he was looking for an excuse to spend more time with her? A flattering possibility.

She told him the cost, and he nodded. "Yeah, I'd like to participate. I'm sure I'll learn a lot."

"You teach high school, right?"

He nodded again. "I teach math. I have a few summer projects going, but I'm free on Tuesdays, fortunately. What do I have to do to sign up?"

"Just show up at the inn next Tuesday at six. I warn you, I don't have your training in teaching, so the classes will be very informal. And you'll be the only man in the group."

"I can deal with that," he said with a laugh.

She had a feeling he'd be the most popular member of the class.

She gave him her card with her cell phone number… in case he thought of any questions beforehand, she explained casually. Finishing her drink, she glanced at her watch. "I'd better get those vegetables home before they start roasting in the car. Thank you for the coffee, Paul. I enjoyed talking with you."

"Same here." He stood as she did. "I'll look forward to next Tuesday. I'm sure you have a lot to teach me."

She felt her eyebrows rise a bit in response to his tone—had there been a bit of a flirtatious undertone?—but then she decided she was probably overanalyzing. Of course he referred only to cooking skills.

She had the sense that he watched her walk away, though she didn't look back to make sure. She found herself smiling during the drive home, her pulse fluttering a little. Was she looking forward to next Tuesday just a bit too much?

She was probably too young for him. Paul didn't know how old Bonnie Carmichael was, but she didn't look much older than his daughter. He wasn't quite sure if Bonnie thought of him as anything more than the father of a bride. A dad who had a lamentable habit of crashing into her.

He'd been startled enough by the physical impact with her the first time they'd met. But then he'd looked down at her and had been metaphorically jolted again. She was so pretty, in the classic sense of the word. Big blue eyes framed by long lashes, a perfect nose and chin, a fair, heart-shaped face framed by wavy blond hair. Not very tall, but nicely curved. His first thought had been a simple "Wow."

Maybe she'd had coffee with him today only to sign him up for her class, but she'd seemed to enjoy the conversation, and the invitation to join had seemed spontaneous. He had talked an awful lot about himself, he recalled with a grimace as he dumped the four squash he'd purchased into the crisper drawer of his nearly empty fridge, hardly desirable dating etiquette. Not that having an impromptu coffee with Bonnie counted as a date, of course. But maybe she wouldn't mind getting together again, if he hadn't bored her senseless with his life history.

Not that he was looking for anything serious, of course. Only a few weeks away from having a grown, married daughter, free to put his desires first for the first time since he was a teenager, he certainly wasn't eager to tie himself down to a serious relationship before the wedding even took place. Especially not with anyone looking to get married and have kids—the stage of life he figured was already in his past. Women Bonnie's age were often thinking along those lines, but he'd gotten the impression that she was more concerned at the moment with getting the inn on a solid financial footing. Which meant maybe she would be interested in spending a little time just having fun with someone else who wasn't looking for more?

The outside kitchen door opened and his daughter hurried in. Cassie always rushed, even when she had no place to be. He always teased that she'd bypassed crawling as a baby and had progressed straight into running. With only a few weeks remaining until her wedding and with her fiancé already spending much of his time in London, his daughter had moved in with him two weeks ago when the lease on her apartment had expired. She could have moved back in with her mother's family, of course, but his place was closer to the university she attended, and she claimed that her mother's place was too hectic with fourteen-year-old twins always in and out with their friends. Paul had been delighted to welcome her to his home until the wedding, giving him a chance to savor this time with her before she moved so far away.

"I hope you haven't eaten lunch," she said, hefting a paper bag. "I stopped for a takeout salad on the way here and I bought you one, too. Whoa, are those fresh vegetables you're putting away? You've been buying produce?"

"I went to the farmers' market," he told her, feeling somewhat sanctimonious as he closed the fridge. "I bought peaches, tomatoes, squash and a loaf of banana nut bread made by a local bakery."

"The banana bread is an indulgence, of course, but the fruit and veggies are a nice step forward for you. I'm proud of you," she teased, setting the takeout bag on the central island in his tidy kitchen.

"You're about to be thoroughly impressed," he assured her gravely. "I've signed up for cooking classes. Six hours of instruction on cooking with seasonal produce."

Cassie made a show of slapping her hands to her cheeks, her bright green eyes rounded, her rosy mouth shaped into an O of surprise. Her layered strawberry blond hair bounced around her face with her energetic movements. "You're taking cooking lessons? What has gotten into you?"

He shrugged. "You won't be around after August to nag me about eating healthier. I guess it'll be up to me to take care of myself."

"I guess you're right." She stood on tiptoe to brush her lips across his cheek. "But I'll still call all the time from London to make sure you're being good. Every day, maybe."

"I hope so." Despite his light tone, he still couldn't think of her being that far away without a hollow feeling in his midsection.

"Who's offering these classes? The community college?"

Filling two glasses with ice, he shook his head. "Bonnie Carmichael will be teaching them at Bride Mountain Inn. I ran into her—er, sort of literally—at the farmers' market this morning and one thing led to another and before I knew it I was signed up for cooking classes."

"Please tell me you didn't knock her down again," Cassie said with a groan, looking up from setting out their salads on the round oak kitchen table.

He laughed ruefully. "Just bumped her arm and knocked a tomato out of her hand. Wasn't my fault this time. Some woman nearly ran me over trying to get to a basket of cucumbers."

"Honestly, Dad, this woman is hosting my wedding. If you keep assaulting her, she's going to fire me as a client."

Though he knew Cassie was teasing, he shook his head. "She's much too professional to take it out on you. I could tell how much pride she takes in the inn."

"Yes, so could I. Kinley's really ambitious for the inn too, I think, but from what I've seen, Bonnie is the one who just truly loves the place, you know? I get the impression that for Kinley it's a career. One she loves, but still a job. For Bonnie, the inn is her home. Definitely where her heart is."

From the time she was a young teen, Cassie had prided herself on being an astute observer of people. She was so good at it that her friends often consulted her about potential dates—and she boasted that she'd saved a few from making big mistakes. Paul thought she was right on the money this time. From what he'd observed of the Carmichael sisters, his daughter had just perfectly summed up their feelings about their family inn. He hadn't spent any time with Logan Carmichael, so he couldn't say what Bonnie's brother felt about the place, but he'd seen the love in Bonnie's eyes when she'd talked about the inn where she lived and worked.

He'd never really felt that connection to a place. Home to him for the past twenty-one years had been where his daughter was. Now that she was moving away he was going to have to find a new definition for himself. There was a certain freedom in the knowledge that after August there was nothing holding him here, no reason not to strike out and explore the world a bit on his own, as his predominantly married, tied-down friends had pointed out to him lately. Footloose traveling was something he'd never felt he could do—never wanted to do—while Cassie was growing up.

"I still can't believe you're going to take cooking classes," Cassie commented as she stabbed a fork into her takeout grilled chicken salad. "I mean, it's great—but funny."

"Bonnie warned me I'll be the only man. It's a small class. Only six students."

His daughter grinned. "Maybe you'll meet someone interesting there. Someone single, nice…and a healthy cook, as a bonus."

Cassie had been trying to fix him up with someone for quite a while, but especially since she'd become engaged. He suspected she was afraid he'd be lonely after she moved away. And maybe he would, at least at first…but he'd deal with it, he thought in dry amusement. He didn't need his kid to find companionship for him. Nor did he see any reason to mention to her that the most intriguing part of the class for him at the moment was the fact that pretty Bonnie Carmichael was the teacher.

"So did you pick up your wedding programs yet?" he asked her, abruptly changing the subject.

Her face lit up. The one sure way to distract Cassie from any uncomfortable subject was to ask about her wedding preparations. "Yes, this morning. They're so pretty! Exactly what I wanted to hand out at the wedding, with the poem Mike and I love so much printed at the top and very cool, stylized flowers as a border. I left them at Mom's house, but I brought one home to show you. I think I left it in the car. I'll run out and get it when I finish my salad. I'm so glad I decided to go with pistachio and dove-gray for my wedding colors, even though Mom was concerned about the combination. It's going to be gorgeous, Dad. Really."

"I have no doubt." His design-major daughter had impeccable tastes, if not as traditional as her mother would have liked.

"And just to make Mom happy, I'm adding a few pops of coral here and there," she confided.

"You know your mother will like anything you decide for your wedding. She just wants you to be happy. As do I."

"I know." She smiled somewhat mistily at him. "I'm so lucky to have you as parents, Daddy. I want you to know I'm aware that you've both always put my best interests ahead of your own. Someday, when Mike and I have kids, I hope we'll be nearly as good at parenting as you two have been."

He cleared his throat with what Cassie would probably have termed his typical male awkwardness at such a blatantly sentimental moment. "At least you and Mike are getting married and establishing your careers before diving into parenthood. Your mom and I did the best we could considering we were just dumb kids ourselves."

"And you learned to change diapers and braid hair and kiss boo-boos while other guys your age were chilling at college keg parties," she teased fondly. "Mom told me you never missed even one of your visitation weekends even when you spent all week juggling work and college, nor did you hesitate to babysit any time she needed a break. And you never complained about child support payments. In fact, she said you often slipped her a little extra when you had it."

Hearing her describing his life since his late teens served as a reminder of the freedom that lay ahead for him. There were parts of it that were going to be very nice, indeed, even though he knew there would be times when he missed those earlier days. Still, he was rather intrigued by the idea of discovering what it would be like to be Paul, the bachelor, rather than just "Cassie's dad." But for the next few weeks he would continue to fill that role willingly and to the best of his abilities.

"Do you need a little extra, Cass? I know the wedding stuff must be getting expensive."

Her laugh pealed musically through his functional little kitchen. "Daddy, I'm not hinting for cash. Trust me, you've paid enough toward the wedding. I'm just trying to thank you for all you've done for me. I don't know, I guess I woke up in a sappy mood this morning. I realized that in just a little over five weeks, I'll be getting married and moving hundreds of miles away from you for the first time in my life. And I don't want to do that without making sure you know exactly how much I love you and how grateful I am to you for giving me such a happy childhood."

"Your mom and Larry had a lot to do with that, too."

"Yes. And I'm thanking both of them for their part. The three of you have been a rare and amazing team. I know it wasn't always easy, and I know it required compromise from all of you—but you did it for me. And for the twins, by the way. They know how lucky they are to have their 'Uncle Paul' in their life."

From across the table, he pointed his fork at her.

"Okay, I'm going to say one thing and then I want to change the subject before I embarrass myself by bursting into unmanly tears here. Regardless of how it came about, you are the best thing that ever happened to me. I knew it from the first time I laid eyes on you, when I was just a scared kid who'd barely started shaving. Yeah, it was hard sometimes, but I wouldn't change one thing that brought us to where we are today. I love you and I am so proud of you. Now, change of topic, please."

Cassie blinked rapidly and gave him a sweet, misty smile. "So, Bonnie Carmichael is really pretty, hmm? I can't help wondering if that has anything to do with your sudden urge to learn about healthy cooking."

Actually, he'd been wondering that, as well.

Chapter Two

At five minutes before six on the following Tuesday, Bonnie mingled politely with the five women who'd assembled for the first of the three cooking classes. She was confident her bright smile hid her foolish disappointment that Paul Drennan hadn't shown up. It wasn't as if she'd really expected him to take the class, despite his impulsive acceptance of her invitation last week. It had been silly to spend so much time thinking about him and hoping she'd get through the classes without making a fool of herself because of her atypical clumsiness around him.

For this first class, she had the students gather for refreshments around one of the tables in the large, sunny dining room of Bride Mountain Inn. China cups and saucers and plates of petits fours and delicate meringues sat in front of them.

Silver candlesticks graced the tables, along with white linens and colorful flowers in crystal vases. An antique silver plate and crystal chandelier gleamed overhead. Great-grandmother Finley had salvaged that piece from an old Virginia plantation when she and her husband originally opened the inn in the 1930s, and it had hung here since with only occasional refurbishing, most recently when Bonnie and her siblings had taken ownership. Bonnie had insisted on keeping as many of the original furnishings and decorations as possible during the remodel. They'd restored almost all of the beautiful old light fixtures. Given the value of these items, they limited their guests to ages twelve and older, directing callers with smaller children to nice family motels and inns nearby.

Kinley and Logan both had other part-time jobs—Kinley selling real estate, Logan consulting for business software design—but Bonnie's whole life was here at the inn. She worked here seven days a week, and she hadn't even taken a real vacation in the past three years. As far as she was concerned, teaching this class was just another task that went along with her responsibilities as hostess, head chef, housekeeper, decorator and concierge. Kinley called her "the heart of the inn." Bonnie rather liked that title.

Standing beside the demonstration table she had prepared, she cleared her throat to claim the attention of the chattering group of friends. "I think we're almost ready to start. Some of you may want to move to another table so everyone can see clearly. Before we begin, does anyone need a refill on coffee, tea, lemonade or water?"

The women gathered their snacks and arranged

themselves around two tables, their noisy conversations barely abating in the process. Bonnie wondered if she could get this ebullient group quiet long enough to teach them anything. Nora Willis, the woman who'd persuaded Bonnie to offer this class for her group of thirtysomething friends, was the loudest of them all, her frequent, hearty laughter filling the room.

With one minute remaining until six o'clock, Bonnie drew a deep breath and spoke above the happy din. "If everyone is comfortable, we'll go ahead and—"

Paul rushed into the room with a sheepish smile and an apology. "I'm sorry I'm late. Please forgive me for the interruption."

Bonnie was glad everyone had turned to look at the newcomer rather than at her. It gave her a moment to ensure that her expression didn't give away her pleasure at seeing him enter, all windblown, flustered and sexy male.

Teaching this class had just become considerably more difficult. Not because she didn't know the subject matter, but because it would be all too easy for Paul Drennan to become the teacher's pet.

Paul settled into a chair at the second table, greeting the two women there quickly with smiles and nods, all the while looking apologetically at Bonnie. She smiled to assure him she wasn't annoyed, then addressed the group again. "Most of you know each other, but for our newcomer's sake, why don't you go around the tables and introduce yourselves. Nora, you start."

Nora and her four friends took turns stating their names, looking directly at Paul as they did so. Nora, Lydia, Kathy, Jennifer and Heather were visibly pleased to have an attractive man in the group—especially

Lydia and Jennifer, who were both divorced. Paul just happened to sit at the same table as the two singles, and they seemed delighted to have him there. Tall, artfully ombre-haired Jennifer, in particular, appeared to be more intrigued by her new classmate than the cooking lessons. Bonnie didn't miss noting that Jennifer scooted her chair a bit closer to Paul's as if to hear him better when he introduced himself.

Bonnie began the class by passing out copies of the syllabus they would follow during this and the next two sessions. Each syllabus was tucked into a bright red pocket folder which she informed them would be filled by the end of the course with useful handouts and website suggestions. Incorporating Nora's requests, she'd divided the three two-hour classes into one-hour blocks: Introduction to Seasonal Cooking; Fresh Herbs; Knife Skills; Spring and Summer Recipes; Fall and Winter Recipes; Canning, Drying and Freezing.

"I'll be at the farmers' market next Tuesday morning at eight," she added as she distributed the schedules. "For those who are free and would like to join me, we can shop together for ingredients for the dishes we'll make that evening."

"I can meet you there after I drop off the kids at day camp," Jennifer said eagerly. "It sounds like fun, doesn't it, Paul?"

"Yes, it does." He smiled up at Bonnie when she gave him his handout, and she wondered if it was only an accident that his fingers brushed hers as he accepted it. Whether intentional or not, that fleeting contact still made her hand tingle. She flexed her fingers surreptitiously as she returned to the demo table to begin her informal lecture about the many advantages—ecologically, financially and nutritionally—of cooking with fresh, locally grown produce.

She tried very hard to divide her attention evenly among the class members. She made a point not to look at Paul too much—or too little, which could be just as noticeable. She didn't like feeling so self-conscious, and she chided herself mentally for her schoolgirl behavior. But still she was too keenly aware of him sitting there listening so attentively, even when other members of the class called attention to themselves with blurted comments or questions or jests. Jennifer, in particular, seemed intent on making sure Paul knew she was available for extracurricular activities.

After forty minutes of lecture and discussion, Bonnie suggested a ten-minute break before the next session. "Feel free to walk in the gardens or help yourself to snacks and drinks, but please keep an eye on the time so we can begin again promptly."

Taking advantage of the cooler temperatures as shadows lengthened in the gardens, the women decided to step outside for the break while Bonnie set up for the next session. "Come with us, Paul," Jennifer urged. "The gardens here are just beautiful."

"Yes, I've seen them and they are," he replied with an easy smile. "But I need to speak with Bonnie for a moment before class starts again."

Seeming unable to come up with a reason to linger with him, Jennifer went out with the others, though she looked back over her shoulder at Paul before stepping outside. Paul waited until the door had closed before reaching into his pocket and pulling out a check. "My registration fee," he said. "Wouldn't want you to think I'm a freeloader."

Bonnie laughed and tucked the check into a deep pocket of her floral summer skirt. "I didn't think that."

"I'm not really in the mood to walk the gardens right now. Is there anything I can do to help you set up for the next part?"

He was too much the gentleman to admit that he was avoiding Jennifer, but Bonnie had her suspicions. "You can bring things in from the kitchen, if you like," she said.

Maybe he was just being polite, genuinely attempting to be helpful rather than trying to escape the attentions of an admittedly attractive woman. The awkward truth was, she hadn't much liked seeing Jennifer flirting so blatantly with Paul, but maybe he'd liked it very much. It would certainly be unprofessional of her to flirt with him, at least while he was a participant in her class, she told herself primly.

And still she found herself smiling up at him through her lashes when he stopped close beside her in the kitchen. "You can carry one basket," she said, motioning toward the two large picnic-style baskets on the counter. "I'll get the other one."

"I'd be happy to." He reached for the closest handle. "I'm sorry again that I was so late," he said as they carried the baskets into the dining room. "The twins needed a lift to a youth party at their church and their mom got hung up at work and everyone else was otherwise occupied, so she called me. I'd have still had plenty of time, but Jenna had to try on every pair of shoes in her closet before she decided she was ready to go. I have to admit I was pretty impatient with her by the time we finally got away, because I was really looking forward to this class."

"You were exactly on time," she reminded him, then asked, "Jenna is one of the twins, right?"

"Right. Jenna and Jackson."

Setting her basket on the demo table, Bonnie glanced up at him, thinking not for the first time that he had a decidedly different relationship with his daughter's other family. She couldn't help wondering, though, why he'd never started a new family of his own. He seemed to enjoy fatherhood—even honorary "unclehood"—but she'd heard no evidence of a special woman in his life. Was he a commitment-phobe? Or—she couldn't help frowning a little—was he still hung up on his remarkable ex after all these years, even though Holly had long since moved on? Not that it was any of her business, of course.

He stood back and watched as she unloaded the supplies onto the demo table. She unpacked six cute little glass jars with home-printed labels, arranging them next to a food processor. Paul picked up one of the jars and read the label. "You're making pesto?"

"Yes. Everyone's going home with a jar tonight and easy instructions for making it yourself."

He chuckled and replaced the jar. "Now that would impress Cassie, if I served her pesto I made myself."

Laughing softly, Bonnie patted his arm without thinking about it. "By the time you've finished this class, you can wow her with a whole meal you prepared yourself, from the salad course to dessert, all made with fresh, local produce."

He rested his hand over hers before she could draw away and gave a little squeeze to her fingers. "She'll think you're a miracle worker."

Though his gesture had been casual, teasing, as had

her own, she reacted as she had before to his touch. Or rather, she overreacted with a surge of awareness and a wave of heat that were totally out of proportion to the situation. Quickly drawing her hand away on the pretext of setting out more supplies, she told herself that she really had neglected her social life for too long. Maybe she'd start working on that online dating profile this very evening, though she wondered if she would find anyone there as interesting and appealing as Paul.

Jennifer came back into the dining room, followed closely by the others. Jennifer made a beeline for Paul. "You missed a lovely walk in the garden," she said. "It's cooler now that the sun's gone down a bit, and the flowers are beautiful. And that fountain…well, it's just perfect."

"What he really missed was the look on Heather's face when that big dog suddenly appeared beside the fountain," Nora said with a giggle that was too deliberately girlish for her age. "That was priceless."

Heather scowled. "Well, you have to admit he looked scary. I couldn't help that little gasp. Thank goodness I saw almost immediately that he was being held by his owner."

Bonnie swallowed a groan. "That's my brother's dog, Ninja. I know he looks intimidating, but he's really very gentle. And Logan keeps him on a leash when they take their walks around the property."

Logan had learned to keep the curious rottweiler-mix dog under close supervision because of Ninja's uncanny knack for escaping all but the most secure enclosures. Ninja was completely harmless, rarely even barked, but his size alone was enough to frighten nervous guests, so he was not allowed to freely roam the grounds. When Logan was busy, Ninja was locked into the sizeable backyard of Logan's cottage down the hill from the inn. The two could often be seen taking long walks around the property early in the mornings and late in the day, good exercise for both of them. Logan had bonded with the former stray in a way he rarely did with people, other than his two sisters.

"You said the dog's owner is your brother?" Lydia asked a bit too casually. "He's a nice-looking man, isn't he?"

Smiling a little, Bonnie said, "Yes, I think so."

"Single?"

"Very."

"You Carmichael siblings," Nora said with a teasing shake of her head. "All work, all the time. At least Kinley is in a romantic relationship now, but I'm beginning to wonder if you and Logan are married to this inn."

"Let's just say we've made the inn our top priority for the past few years," Bonnie replied lightly. "We'll get around to other things, eventually."

She glanced at her watch and then motioned toward the tables. "We should get started again. Who would like to volunteer to be my assistant during this next segment?"

"I volunteer Paul." Nora shot a mischievous grin at her only male classmate. "I think he'd look especially cute in an apron."

If Nora had hoped to see him embarrassed, her teasing gambit failed. Paul accepted the challenge with alacrity. "I'd be happy to help," he said, moving around the table to stand beside Bonnie.

Bonnie donned a red-and-white gingham, bib-style apron embroidered on the center pocket with the Bride

Mountain Inn logo. She tied a loose bow behind her back, then smiled as she picked up a matching apron for Paul. "This will be a little short for you, but it will keep you from splashing oil or pesto on your clothes."

While the rest of the class grinned appreciatively, he bent to allow her to slip the top loop over his head. His face was very close to hers as she did so, and she couldn't resist looking at his mouth. He had such a nice mouth. His eyes met hers for a moment and the glint in them made her wonder uncomfortably if he had read her thoughts. But then he straightened and turned so she could secure the ties behind his back. His strong, straight back. With a firm, tight…

Clearing her throat abruptly, she turned back toward the demo table. "Fresh herbs, whether grown in your own kitchen garden or purchased from the market, are a must for any home chef," she began, greatly relieved that her voice sounded reasonably normal to her ears.

Now if only she could get through the rest of this demonstration without making an utter fool of herself. Considering how distracting she found her handsome assistant, it was going to take all her concentration.

Paul hoped the handouts Bonnie had provided contained all the information he needed to glean from her class. As hard as he'd tried to pay attention to her lectures and demonstrations, he couldn't guarantee he'd remember half of what she'd said. Not because the class hadn't been interesting or because Bonnie wasn't knowledgeable about her subject. Every time he tried to pay close attention to her words, he found himself noticing how soft and musical her voice was, how much he enjoyed just listening to her. And every time he focused intently on her face, he got lost in admiring her big blue eyes, her porcelain skin, the tiny dimple just at the right corner of her mouth.

So, just how long had it been since he'd even been on a date with a woman? Obviously too long, judging by his strong and decidedly physical reactions to Bonnie Carmichael's many charms. He'd had a brief association with Michaela Havers close to a year ago, but that had lasted only a few months. They'd had different interests, different friends, different priorities. Outside the bedroom—where they'd gotten along well enough—their interactions had become awkward and forced, until by mutual agreement they'd called it off. He'd seen her at a party recently. She'd been with a new guy and had looked very happy. They'd chatted amiably for a few minutes, parting as friendly acquaintances, if not actually friends.

He seemed to have a knack for remaining on cordial terms with his exes, he thought wryly. He didn't want to analyze too deeply what that said about his potential for long-term commitment, something that seemed less likely with each passing year. Since Michaela, there'd been a few pleasant evenings out with other women, but nothing serious, no uncomfortable expectations on either part. But it had been a while since he'd even done that.

He wasn't sure he had any more in common with Bonnie Carmichael than he'd had with Michaela, yet still he buzzed like a live wire every time he was close to her. He didn't want either of them to get burned by that electricity, but from what she'd said to Nora, it didn't sound as though Bonnie was looking for anything serious right now, either. Made sense. She was young, busy and ambitious with her plans for the inn. She had plenty of time to think about starting a family in a couple of years, perhaps, once she was satisfied the inn was secure. At this point, she was probably just wishing for a little fun away from work sometimes.

He liked having fun, too. And if he and Bonnie could share some good times together, without either of them thinking wedding bells and baby booties, all the better.

Somehow, despite his wandering thoughts about the teacher, he made it through the demonstration without chopping his fingers along with the basil, or blowing up the food processor, or breaking any of the delicate little jars she'd provided for the pesto samples. To good-natured applause from his classmates, he took a bow at the conclusion of the session.

Dismissed by Bonnie with a reminder of the farmers' market visit next Tuesday, the women gathered their belongings and moved toward the doorway, still talking and laughing. A garrulous group, but affable, he thought. They'd made him feel quite welcome this evening.

The friendliest member of the class lingered when the others departed. Her long, lean body nicely displayed in a formfitting summer dress, Jennifer took her time storing her pesto, class folder and cell phone in her canvas tote bag. "Looks like we're the last ones," she said to Paul, as if that were a surprise to her. "We can walk out together to our cars."

He supposed he should be flattered by her attention. She was certainly attractive, though he noticed only in an objective, rather detached manner. He didn't mind her blatant flirting. He wasn't the type of man who thought the male should always be the instigator. He actually enjoyed being asked out—unless he wasn't interested, in which case he always felt bad about declining. He wasn't interested now, so he hoped he was wrong about Jennifer's intentions.

He glanced at tiny, curvy Bonnie, and his pulse rate jumped in a way it hadn't when Jennifer smiled at him. There was the primary explanation for his lack of interest in Jennifer. His gaze met Bonnie's, and he saw what he thought was understanding cross her face.

"Paul isn't leaving just yet," she said with a smile for him. "He and I need to discuss something about his daughter's upcoming wedding."

Jennifer blinked slowly a couple of times as she looked at Paul again. "Your, um, daughter?"

He nodded. "Cassie's having her wedding here at the inn in just over a month. Bonnie's been a tremendous help to us."

"I see. Well, I'm sure that's been keeping you very busy lately."

Paul laughed lightly. "Cassie's been keeping me busy for the past twenty-one years."

"Do you have any other kids?"

"No, just the one. In just a few weeks, I'll be a contented empty-nester."

Jennifer looked somewhat speculatively from him to Bonnie and back again, then gave a little shrug. "I'm off, then. See you both next week. Great class tonight, Bonnie."

"Thank you. I'm glad you enjoyed it." Bonnie waited until Jennifer had let herself out before turning to Paul. "I hope I read the look you gave me correctly. You did want an excuse to stay a few minutes longer, didn't you?"

"I did," he confessed. Maybe he had misinterpreted, but he thought he'd seen the expression on Jennifer's face before—recently divorced single mom looking to fill a position he had no interest in auditioning for. He hoped she'd gotten that message, if he'd been right about her initial interest in him. "She seems very nice, but…"

Bonnie merely nodded and started gathering the supplies from the class. He knew she was much too ethical to discuss one of her other students with him. To justify staying behind, he helped her clean up.

"How *are* the wedding arrangements coming along?" Bonnie asked as they carried the supplies into the kitchen. "Do you know of anything Cassie needs from us at the moment?"

He wasn't sure if she was simply making small talk or keeping him honest about his excuse to stay a bit longer. He was amused by his suspicion that it was mostly the latter. "As far as I can determine, everything's on track. She told me her dress is almost finished and all the decisions have been made and orders have been placed. Now it's just a matter of getting through all the showers and parties scheduled for the next few weeks—and she still has four and a half weeks of school to complete."

The last of those showers would actually take place here at the inn, he remembered. Cassie had mentioned that her bridesmaids had met with Bonnie and Kinley and booked the dining room for the first Sunday afternoon in August, a week and six days before the big event. Somewhat late for a shower, Holly had said with typical disapproval at the lack of efficient organization, but Cassie had only laughed and said her friends were all busy young professionals and students and they'd booked the only day they could manage. Besides, she had reminded her mom, she hadn't exactly given everyone a lot of notice. Cassie and Mike hadn't even chosen a wedding date until mid-May, only three months before the event.

"I'm so impressed that she's actually making her own dress from her own design," Bonnie marveled.

"Oh, yeah, she's a whiz with a sewing machine."

"Sounds like a busy time for her. How's she holding up?"

He chuckled. "My Cassie is not easy to rattle. She goes with the flow. She'd consider a wedding disaster just another great story to tell her kids someday."

"Oh, how I wish more brides had that attitude," Bonnie said as she closed a cabinet door.

"I suppose you've seen your share of meltdowns."

Her smile was wry. "A few, and I'm sure I'll see many more in the future."

She was optimistic about the long-term success of her establishment, he noted. An admirable attitude, reminding him how very attached she was to the inn. How deeply she'd planted her roots here.

"Cassie made all her friends promise that if they saw even a glimmer of 'Bridezilla' making an appearance in her, they were to give her a swift kick in the butt."

Bonnie laughed softly. "That's cute. So many brides act like one little glitch in their obsessively detailed plans will ruin their lives forever."

She bit her lip suddenly, looking as though she wasn't sure if she'd stepped over a professional line.

"Of course, we do our best here to make sure all our events go as smoothly as our clients desire," she assured him.

Trying to hide his amusement, he nodded solemnly. "Surely you don't get blamed for things that are out of your control."

Forgetting herself again, she rolled her eyes. "A bride once threatened to sue us because it rained on her wedding day."

"You're kidding."

Shaking her head with a pained sigh, she said, "I wish I was. She also blamed her groom, her mother and God, in that order after us, and spent an hour crying in the ladies' room before we could coax her out after the brief rain shower ended. She ended up having a very nice, if a bit damp, wedding."

"So that's why you spell out in your contract that you aren't responsible for weather or other acts of nature. Cassie thought that was funny."

"More like a necessity. Can you put this container on that shelf, please? The top one?"

Obligingly, he slid the lidded plastic box easily onto a shelf well above Bonnie's head.

"Thank you. You saved me from having to pull out the stepladder."

Glancing at the high cabinets lining the no-wasted-space kitchen, he smiled. He was unable to resist patting the top of her blond head, which came just about level with his shoulder. "I have a feeling you spend a lot of time with that stepladder."

She grinned up at him. "Are you kidding? If I ever get married, it'll be one of my attendants."

Even though it was only a joke, her reference to

marriage made him automatically drop his hand and take a half step back from her. He tried to cover his foolish reaction by opening the second basket for unpacking. "Are there any other high shelves I can reach for you before I go?"

"As a matter of fact…" Seemingly oblivious to his awkward moment, she had him store several more items.

"I hope this gets me extra points in the class."

Wiping her hands on a kitchen towel, she smiled. "You know I'm not grading the class."

That fleeting little dimple at the corner of her mouth could make a man's mouth go dry. He swallowed before murmuring, "Still…"

Draping the towel over a rack, she pushed back her hair and said, "I think it's safe for you to go now. The parking lot should be empty. Thank you for your help."

"I wasn't afraid to go out with the class," he said with exaggerated male dignity. "I just, uh, thought you could use a hand."

As he'd hoped, she laughed again. She had such a pretty laugh, soft and musical. His lips quirked automatically upward in response and he bade her goodnight with a smile. If he fantasized about parting with a kiss—well, he assured himself as he headed for his car, that was only natural considering his attraction to her. Because he sensed the attraction wasn't entirely one-sided, he hoped maybe someday soon that fantasy could come true.

Darkness had settled fully over the grounds by the time Bonnie headed out of the inn that night. After class she'd checked on the guests playing board games in the shared front parlor, and did some prep for breakfast the next morning. Finally deciding to call it a day, she slipped out a back door onto the long wooden deck where an older couple who were staying a few days to celebrate their fifty-first wedding anniversary sat in rockers, sipping tea and enjoying the moonlight. She exchanged good-nights with them, but didn't linger, leaving them to their quiet companionship.

Rather than heading straight into her half basement apartment, she turned at the foot of the stairs and walked along one of the graveled paths toward the back of the gardens. She needed a few minutes of fresh air to clear her head before turning in for the night. The lighting was sufficient to safely guide her steps, but not so bright as to dim the beauty of the star-studded sky overhead. Not that she needed lighting at all. She could walk every inch of the inn's grounds with her eyes closed.

The gardens spreading around the gray-painted, white-trimmed Queen-Anne style inn had been designed to be inviting, peaceful and reasonably low-maintenance with well-tended pathways winding through the flower beds. A large, three-tier fountain was the central attraction, with a white-painted wedding gazebo at the east side of the grounds. The east side lawn had been leveled, providing space for tents or tables and chairs for outdoor parties and receptions. Stone steps and a wheelchair ramp led down from that lawn to the lower gardens.

As she walked, Bonnie saw both the beauty of the grounds and the many backbreaking, blister-raising, sweat-drenching hours of manual labor she and her siblings had put into the restoration. They had helped their uncle Leo as often as they could, but they'd been busy establishing careers in Tennessee, so there'd been a lot of work to do when they'd officially inherited the place. Bonnie regretted none of it, and she was confident Kinley and Logan felt the same.

She paused at the back of the grounds, just before the trailhead of a hiking path that led through dense woods to the peak of Bride Mountain. They eventually planned to do a bit more development here, hoping to create a quiet meditation garden complete with a koi pond.

Movement to her right made her turn. A massive dark shape separated from the shadows to bump against her, a low rumble issuing from its throat. The dog's head came higher than her waist, so she didn't even have to bend to give him an affectionate pat on the head. He growled louder when she rubbed his ears, a sound that she'd always thought of as Ninja's version of a purr. The dog almost never barked, but he made this sound frequently, leading some wary observers to think he was growling at *them*.

"I thought you and Ninja had already made your rounds for the evening," she said to her brother.

His hard-carved face mostly in shadow, Logan Carmichael would probably have appeared intimidating to anyone who didn't love him as much as his younger sister did. "Guess we're both restless tonight. Nothing good on TV."

"You want to come in for cake and tea? I have a little left of that coconut cake I made for dinner last night."

"Thanks, but not tonight. Ninja and I are just going to walk the trail a bit."

Looking up from the dog, she raised an eyebrow at her brother. "Hiking in the dark?"

"Not a hike. Just a short walk. There's enough moonlight to guide us. And I've got a flashlight if needed."

"Still…"

He chuckled and lightly flicked the end of her nose. "Afraid your ghost will get me?"

She rolled her eyes. Her brother and sister had always teased her about being the only one in the family who believed the more-than-a-century-old legend that a ghostly bride was occasionally seen on the grounds of the inn, almost always glimpsed by couples on the verge of committing to happily-ever-after. Uncle Leo swore that he and Aunt Helen had seen the bride the night he proposed. They had enjoyed a blissfully happy marriage until her death had parted them.

Since Kinley had tumbled into love recently with travel writer Dan Phelan, she had been quieter on the subject of the ghost bride, about whom she'd once had very strong—and somewhat negative—opinions. Kinley had been concerned that having a ghost legend attached to their newly reopened inn would be a negative factor, garnering the wrong sort of attention or discouraging the wedding clientele they hoped to attract. Now she merely got a funny look on her face on the infrequent occasion when the bride was mentioned. But characteristically gruff and pragmatic Logan still managed to get in a few cynical jabs toward Bonnie's admitted romanticism.

Refusing to take the bait this time, Bonnie simply shrugged and retorted, "I'm more concerned about you *becoming* the next ghost to haunt the inn. Don't fall off any embankments and break your neck while you're out walking off your restlessness, okay?"

"I won't. And if I do, I promise to haunt you only on your birthdays and Christmas."

Laughing softly at his rare joke, Bonnie pushed her hands into her skirt pockets as she watched man and dog disappear into the dark woods. Something crinkled crisply against her right hand and she pulled out the check Paul had given her. Glancing down at it, she smoothed the paper slowly between her fingers, thinking of Paul's distinctive jade eyes and charming, slightly crooked smile.

The more time she spent with him, the more she liked him. Though she'd tried to be more subtle than Jennifer, she thought she'd made it clear enough that she wouldn't mind spending more time with him. If her recently reawakened feminine instincts could be trusted, he felt the same way about her. Maybe she'd hold off a bit on that online dating profile.

Something moved at the corner of her vision, this time in the densest part of the woods. Thinking it might be her brother and his dog, she turned, but saw nothing there but the thinnest line of late-night mist. She shook her head, deciding she must be more tired from the long day than she'd realized.

Holding Paul's check tightly in one hand, she headed for her apartment, telling herself she should put him out of her mind for the rest of the night. As if that were possible.

Chapter Three

The woman who sat across the coffee shop table from Paul Thursday afternoon was gym-toned and impeccably styled, not a blond hair out of place, her makeup subtle but perfect. Though he knew her to be only fifteen months from turning forty, Holly Bauer looked a good half decade younger. In fact, she'd been mistaken for twenty-one-year-old Cassie's older sister rather than her mother.

Appearing to be a polar opposite to his sleek, fashionable wife, Holly's husband, Larry, was pudgy and habitually rumpled, with a shiny, balding head and kind, twinkling brown eyes. He had a brilliant mind, a generous heart and an infectious smile. Holly adored him, as did Cassie. Paul was fond of the guy, as well.

Holly sipped delicately from her coffee—black, no sugar—then set the cup on the table. "So, anyway," she said, continuing the solemn conversation they'd been engaged in for the past fifteen minutes, "I thought you should be told right away. And I believed I should be the one to tell you, rather than Cassie. After all, this move will affect you, too, in a way."

"In a rather big way," he agreed, tugging at the open neck of his polo shirt which felt as though it had somehow tightened. "I'll miss you guys."

Holly had just informed him that she and her family would be relocating in August, only a week after Cassie's wedding. Holly had accepted an offer from a law firm in Dallas and Larry was taking a faculty position teaching in the engineering department at UT Dallas. The twins were understandably nervous about changing high schools and leaving their friends, but also excited about moving to Texas. Paul had known the move was a possibility, but now Holly had confirmed that it had become a reality.

"We'll miss you, too," she said with a sincerity he didn't doubt. "The first question Jenna asked when we told them was whether you'll be moving, too."

He supposed he could understand Jenna's assumption. After all, twelve years ago he'd followed the family to Virginia from North Carolina, where he and Holly had both grown up, when Holly and Larry had moved here for Larry's career. Without close family of his own, there'd been no reason for Paul to remain in North Carolina rather than settle close to his daughter. He'd found a teaching position very quickly, bought a nice little house with three extra bedrooms for when Cassie and her siblings visited overnight, and he'd been happy here as part of their extended family. But as much as he cared for them, he couldn't see himself following them to Dallas. Not with his daughter married and living in London.

He forced a smile for Holly's benefit, hoping it looked natural. "I won't be moving to Dallas."

Holly nodded as if she had expected that decision. "It's going to be hard to say goodbye—for all of us," she murmured, just a little tremor in her voice.

Reaching across the table, he took her hand and gave her fingers a squeeze. "It won't be forever," he assured her. "I expect to be invited to the twins' birthday celebrations and graduations, and I'll try to be there if I can get away. And if they want to come back here to visit their friends during vacations and holidays, they'll always have a room in my house."

She squeezed his hand in return before reaching again for her coffee. "It's going to be terribly hectic for the next few weeks, of course," she said, her voice steady again. "Getting ready for the wedding, preparations for the move, and the twins will want to attend as many parties and get-togethers with their friends as they can manage."

"Let me know if there's anything I can do to help."

"Thanks, Paul."

He smiled over the rim of his cup at his daughter's mother. There'd been no romantic feelings between himself and Holly since their youthful infatuation had fizzled away in the stressful reality of teen parenthood, but they'd managed to forge a true friendship during the years. A partnership in a way, dedicated to making sure Cassie had a safe, happy, healthy childhood. It had been quite a successful venture, he mused. But now, as it should, it was coming to an end. Or at the least, it was changing radically. Cassie would always be a bond between them.

"I ran into Michaela Havers at the bank yesterday," Holly commented after a few moments of silence, a seeming non sequitur that made him blink a couple of times before replying.

"Yeah? I saw her at a party not too long ago. She seemed to be doing well."

"She was sporting an engagement ring roughly the size of a golf ball yesterday. A recent development, I take it."

"First I've heard of it," he agreed. "I knew she was seeing someone, but I don't think they were engaged when I saw her last. It all happened pretty quickly, I guess."

"Are you okay with it?"

"Absolutely. Michaela and I broke up by mutual agreement. I wish her the best."

"So…" Holly toyed with the handle of her coffee cup. "Are you seeing anyone special now?"

An image of a pretty, petite blonde popped into his mind. Bonnie wasn't at all like Holly, he mused, other than both being blondes. Holly's sleekly styled bob was colored by an expensive stylist, her makeup was always impeccable and her outfits were tasteful but obviously designer labeled. Bonnie's loose golden curls looked entirely natural, she wore little makeup and her clothes were apparently chosen for comfort and convenience. And while he liked and admired both of them, it was the thought of Bonnie that made his pulse rate pick up even as he shook his head. "Not at the moment."

He eyed Holly with sudden amusement. "Surely you

aren't worried about leaving me behind all alone and sad when you move?"

Maybe her cheeks went just a bit pink as she lifted her chin in denial. "Of course not. You've made a good life for yourself here. I just wondered..."

"Don't worry about me, Holly. I'll be fine. Actually, I guess you could say for the first time in twenty-one years, I'll be free to follow my own whims. I'm pretty much committed to teaching another year here, but after that, maybe I'll teach in China for a couple of years or on a reservation in North Dakota," he said, naming random places off the top of his head. "Or maybe I'll take a sabbatical and spend a year schlepping drinks at some bar in the Florida Keys. I make a mean margarita, you know."

Holly smiled faintly, making no other effort to respond to his grandiose scenarios. Probably because she didn't believe he would do any of them, no matter what he said. Had he become so predictable? He was still young, not even forty. He could have plenty of adventures, if he wanted. China, North Dakota, Florida... anywhere the wind blew him.

After all, he no longer had anything, or anyone, to hold him here.

When they'd reopened Bride Mountain Inn, Bonnie and Kinley had learned quickly that they seemed to attract an early rising clientele, eager to have breakfast and then get on with their planned activities. As a result, Monday through Saturday breakfast service began at seven and formally ended at nine, though Bonnie was well-known to serve the stragglers, anyway.

The daily schedule varied only on Sundays, when a

lavish brunch was served from ten until one. Because Bride Mountain Café, an excellent little diner within walking distance of the inn, was closed on Sundays, Bonnie provided a light repast of sandwiches and dessert for her guests that evening.

The 7:00 a.m. breakfast service necessitated an early start for Bonnie and her full-time housekeeping employee, Rhoda Foley, who cheerfully cleaned, served, cooked, did laundry or whatever else was needed of her, aided by part-time maid Sandy Carr.

Free-spirited, mid-fifties Rhoda had been scrupulously on time every morning since an incident in the spring in which she had overslept, rushed to work and hit one of the front portico posts with her truck, resulting in a mad scramble to make repairs before a scheduled wedding.

With her almost compulsive need for perfection and control, Kinley had been particularly anxious about the damage, though her first reaction had been to make sure Rhoda was unharmed. Minutes after the accident occurred, travel writer Dan Phelan had arrived to profile the inn in a popular Southern-themed magazine, to Kinley's dismay. But since Kinley and Dan had fallen in love almost at first sight and were now a happily committed couple, so Bonnie suspected her sister's memories of that tumultuous day were pleasant ones.

At just after nine Friday morning, Bonnie and Kinley stood near the doorway from the dining room to the kitchen. The inn was fully occupied, mostly with guests for a wedding to take place in the gazebo tomorrow afternoon. Kinley had just arrived, dressed as always in tailored, professional clothing, in contrast to the loose skirts and cotton tops that better suited Bonnie's role at the inn.

To an outside observer, Bonnie knew she and her sister didn't appear to be related. With gold-streaked light brown hair and eyes more gray than blue, Kinley was nearly five inches taller and more athletically built than Bonnie. Both Kinley and Logan resembled their father, while Bonnie had been called the "spitting image" of their mother—perhaps one of the reasons she'd always been great-uncle Leo's favorite. That, and her lifelong passion for the inn he'd loved so much.

Holding a cup of the herbal tea Bonnie had insisted she drink—Bonnie had recently decided that her overachieving, workaholic sister drank entirely too much coffee—Kinley looked around the well-filled dining room in satisfaction. "Your new summer veggie quiche was certainly a hit. Everyone liked it."

Bonnie smiled. "They seemed to. I'll add the recipe to the handouts for my class."

"I had a taste of the quiche. It was delicious. Rosemary?"

"Yes, fresh from my herb garden." The little herb bed Logan had helped her plant was her pride and joy. She was beginning to believe she'd inherited her great-aunt Helen's green thumb along with the inn, even though Helen had been related to her only by marriage to Leo.

Kinley took another taste of her tea before saying, "Speaking of your class, one of your students may be coming by later today."

Bonnie's heart gave a funny little bump. She reminded herself that there were five members of her class in addition to the one who elicited that response. "Oh?"

Looking almost smugly amused, as if she'd sensed the direction in which Bonnie's thoughts had automatically flown, Kinley nodded. "Cassie Drennan called earlier. She's bringing a friend by to see the inn as a potential wedding venue for next spring. She mentioned that her dad might ride along."

So the physical jolt had been justified, after all. It happened again with the confirmation that she would perhaps be seeing Paul that afternoon—even if he had his daughter and her friend with him.

"I'm sure you'll have Cassie's friend signed up for the full package even before they finish looking around," she teased her sister lightly, trying to direct the attention away from herself.

A saleswoman to her core, Kinley grinned. "I'll certainly try. So, you want to be in on the tour? I suspect that Paul—I mean, Cassie—would be happy to have you join us."

"Kinley—"

With a soft laugh, Kinley held up both hands in response to Bonnie's warning mutter. "Sorry. I just think it's so cute the way you blush nearly every time you hear his name."

Cursing her traitorous fair coloring, Bonnie hoped she could get that reaction under control again before Paul arrived.

She changed the subject abruptly to talk of the wedding festivities scheduled for the weekend, a topic sure to distract her sister. Proceeded by a drinks-and-snacks gathering in the dining room, rehearsal was scheduled for seven that evening. A hearty breakfast would be served tomorrow morning to the wedding party, and the big event itself would start at three tomorrow afternoon. The bride had chosen a Tuscan wedding theme, so Logan would be busy today draping rented white columns and the white-painted gazebo with ivy and clusters of artificial grapes. And muttering all the time about how foolish it was to do so, she thought with an indulgent smile, though she knew her brother would do his usual meticulous job.

One other topic was guaranteed to distract Kinley's attention from anything else. "What time is Dan supposed to arrive?" Bonnie asked when there was nothing left to say about the upcoming wedding.

Just the mention of Dan's name made Kinley light up like a Christmas tree, Bonnie noted with a slight sense of wistfulness. "He plans to be here by six, in time for dinner. His last interview for the day should be completed by noon."

As a features writer for the Georgia-based magazine *Modern South,* Dan traveled quite a bit, though he'd shifted his home base to Virginia to be with Kinley. An aspiring political thriller novelist, he hoped in the future to cut back even more on his traveling, though so far they seemed to be doing a great job of melding their busy careers with their private romance.

Kinley glanced at her watch. "Speaking of work, I have to make a couple of calls. I'll catch up with you later."

Bonnie had a lot to do, too. She hoped she'd be much too busy to indulge in daydreams of finding for herself what Kinley had lucked into with Dan.

* * *

Morning chores had been completed when Bonnie stood on the step stool in the kitchen later that afternoon, reaching for a vintage glass punch bowl she stored in one of the higher cabinets. The grape pattern made it perfect for the upcoming wedding's Tuscan theme. She gripped the large bowl carefully between both hands, preparing to descend the ladder, when someone reached up to take the bowl from her. Having been too focused on her task to hear anyone enter the kitchen, she started a bit, but a large hand at her waist kept her safely on the tread.

She looked down to find Paul grinning at her, holding the bowl in the crook of his right arm as he steadied her with his left hand. Even two steps up on the ladder, she was now only an inch or so taller, so their faces were almost level. He looked every bit as good from up here, she decided immediately.

Without disconnecting the contact between them, he set the punch bowl on the counter. "Shouldn't you wait until you have someone to steady you before you climb on ladders?"

"I'm a foot off the floor," she pointed out. "I doubt I'm in danger of breaking my neck."

Her pulse fluttered some when he rested his now-free right hand just above her left hip, so that he held her lightly bracketed between his palms. She felt the warmth of him seeping through her clothing and softening her knees.

Still smiling at her, Paul neither moved away nor made any effort to help her down. He wasn't even pretending now to be securing her on the ladder. And when she placed her hands on his broad shoulders, it wasn't only to steady herself. It seemed time to openly acknowledge the attraction that had simmered between them from the first time they'd collided.

"Your sister is giving Cassie and her friend Danielle a quick tour of the facilities I slipped away on the pretext of asking you about the next cooking class," he confessed.

"You have a question about the class?"

His grin deepened roguishly. "No."

"Oh." She felt her cheeks warm a bit, but attributed the flush more to pleasure than embarrassment.

"I don't mean to keep you from your work," he said with some reluctance.

"I always make time for a visit from a friend," she replied. "But perhaps I should get down from the ladder."

"I don't know. I rather like looking at you from this angle." He focused directly on her mouth as he spoke, and she felt her lips tingle in response.

She glanced automatically toward the open doorway. Had there not been a very good chance that one of her employees could walk in at any moment…

As if sensing the direction of her thoughts, he gave a little sigh, then lifted her easily off the stepladder. The math teacher obviously worked out.

Setting her safely on her feet, he smiled down at her, jade eyes gleaming. "I like looking at you from this angle, too."

Her hands rested on his upper arms now. She cocked her head as she looked up at him. "You're being very flirtatious today."

"I've thought about you a lot the past few days," he confessed.

Hearing those words in his rich, deep voice made her heart do a happy little dance. She had a crush on this guy, she thought. Nice…yet a little scary, too. She didn't want to invest too much, too quickly. She wasn't sure what he had in mind, especially since she thought she'd heard him drop a few clues that he was looking forward to being a carefree bachelor after his daughter's wedding. A "contented empty-nester," as he'd said to Jennifer. Maybe he was just interested in casually spending time together, having a little fun during his summer break.

She wasn't opposed to that, as long as she kept her head—and her heart—somewhat guarded. With her adored mother serving as an example, Bonnie had always been very careful about not giving her heart to a charming commitment-phobe like her father, or like Kinley's selfish first husband. She'd poured all her love into the family and their inn, and had received only joy in return. But it was hard to remain cautious when Paul was just so darned appealing. "You may have crossed my mind a few times," she said.

She could tell he liked that, and he took encouragement to say, "So maybe we could spend more time together? Outside of class, I mean. Maybe a movie? Dinner? I'm going kayaking on the New River with a couple of friends tomorrow. I don't suppose you could get away to join us on such short notice?"

He was asking her out. For some reason she found herself babbling in reply. "My brother likes to kayak the white-water rapids on the New River. I'd love to try it sometime, but I can't tomorrow. We have a wedding in the afternoon."

He released his hold on her and took a half step

back, his smile fading a little. "I won't keep you any longer from your work."

"I could take some time off Monday afternoon or evening, if you're free then," she said quickly, making some quick mental adjustments to her upcoming schedule.

His smile deepened in satisfaction. "Monday sounds great. What time would be best for you?"

They were interrupted before she could reply. With Kinley leading the way, Cassie and her friend Danielle came into the kitchen, looking around curiously. Kinley winked at Bonnie before speaking to Paul. "Cassie wondered where you'd gotten off to. I told her I thought I knew where we might find you. And I was right."

"Dad's developed a sudden interest in kitchens lately," Cassie said with an impish grin that earned her a look from her father.

Bonnie had busied herself folding the step stool and storing it. Only then did she turn to be introduced by Kinley to Danielle Brooks, the prospective client and Cassie's friend. Blessed with the tall, sleek build Bonnie had always envied, Danielle was a beauty with pixie-cut black hair, flawless milk chocolate skin, dancing brown eyes and a thousand-watt smile. Bonnie liked her immediately.

"Danielle and I are in school together," Cassie explained. "We'll both earn our bachelor's degrees next month."

Shaking Danielle's hand, Bonnie asked, "Are you going into fashion design too?"

"Yes. I plan to move to New York next summer, when my fiancé finishes his medical residency here, and I hope to get a job in the fashion industry. In the meantime, I'll be taking some graduate-level courses here at Tech."

"When is the wedding?"

"In the spring. Sometime in May, I think. We haven't booked a venue yet. I want to bring Joe, my fiancé, to tour this place. I think he'll agree that it's perfect."

"I thought so the first time I visited," Cassie endorsed. "Dad agreed, though I'm surprised we weren't banned from the property after he mowed down poor Bonnie—twice! He didn't knock you off the stepladder just now, did he, Bonnie?"

Amused by Paul's irrepressible daughter, Bonnie shook her head. "Actually, he very gallantly helped me down."

"And we are keeping her from her work," Paul inserted smoothly, making Bonnie wonder if he worried about what Cassie might say next. "She and Kinley have a wedding to prepare for."

Cassie nodded. "We saw the decorations their brother and his crew are setting up out in the garden. Looks very Italian."

"That's the goal," Kinley said promptly, still in saleswoman mode. "We do our best to comply with the bride's wishes when it comes to color and theme."

Cassie and Danielle fell into a discussion of all the colors and themes available for spring weddings as Kinley skillfully herded them out of the kitchen and into the dining room.

Paul remained just a minute longer. "So…Monday?"

Bonnie nodded. "Why don't you call me Sunday and we'll set up a time?"

"I'll do that." He winked at her as he left her to her chores.

An image of his roguish smile lingered in her mind throughout the rest of the day—along with the pleasant memory of how good it had felt to be held in his strong arms.

Chapter Four

Though she expected to hear from Paul that weekend, Bonnie was surprised by a call from his daughter late Saturday afternoon. "Hi, Bonnie, it's Cassie Drennan. Is this a bad time to call?"

"No, not at all. I was just taking a break after this afternoon's wedding." Sitting on her couch with her tired, bare feet propped up in front of her, she set aside the glass of iced tea she'd been sipping. "What can I do for you?"

"I do have a favor to ask of you," Cassie confessed. "I wonder if you would mind if I make you a dress?"

Bonnie had been sure Cassie had called about her approaching wedding, and this surprising offer required a mental adjustment. "You want to make a dress for me?"

"Well, I'd like to design and then sew a dress for

you. I need a quick extra credit project for a class, and I came up with the idea of sketching out a petite clothing line. I'll make a dress from one of the sketches, and I'll gift it to you after I've photographed it and submitted it to the professor. Would you mind?"

"No, of course not. I'm flattered that you consider me a suitable model for your design. Or am I just the shortest person you know?" Bonnie added with a laugh.

Cassie chuckled, too. "Of course not. But I would like to experiment with some designs for you. Petite with curves is a very different silhouette than the tall, very thin standard fashion model. A different challenge for a designer. You have a great shape and I'd love to make a great dress for you."

"Aren't you graduating in just a few weeks?"

"I finish four weeks from today, the week before the wedding. Which means I have about ten days to get this done."

"Last-minute decision?"

"In a way. I wasn't sure I'd have time, what with the wedding plans and making my own wedding dress and all, but it turns out I'm somewhat ahead of schedule on everything. I don't really need the extra credit, but if I have too much time on my hands before the wedding, I'll just go crazy, so I thought I'd give this a try, if you're game."

"It sounds like fun," Bonnie said honestly.

"Great. So, when are you free to get together for preliminary measurements? I can come there, or—if it wouldn't be too much trouble—you could come to Dad's house, where I have all my sewing and fitting supplies set up for the next few weeks."

Even as she and Cassie made plans, Bonnie wondered if Paul was aware of this project. And if so, what he thought of having her even more entangled in his family life—at least until after his daughter's wedding.

Sweaty, grass-stained and sore, Paul turned his car into the driveway of his home Sunday afternoon, thinking that maybe he'd overdone it a bit that weekend. Still sunburned from yesterday's kayaking trip, he'd joined several of the same companions and quite a few others today for a rousing game of soccer in a nearby park. His right shin throbbed from a sliding tackle contact that had left a thin smear of dried blood mixed with the dirt on his shorts-bared leg. That tackle had been executed by a female player close to twenty years his junior and maybe a hundred ten pounds soaking wet. He had taken only slim satisfaction in rocketing a hard instep kick straight past her and into the goal a few plays later, after which he'd limped to his team's side and collapsed onto the bench to suck some air into his tired lungs.

He'd held his own, he reminded himself. He was just going to pay for it later, probably a bit more than some of the younger players would. He hadn't been the oldest player on the pitch, but he'd been one of only a few close to forty.

As he pulled into the driveway he noticed an extra car behind Cassie's little economy model. He recognized it with a start. He'd helped Bonnie stash fresh veggies in that car at the farmers' market less than two weeks ago.

What on earth was Bonnie doing here? Parking, he pushed a hand through his tousled hair, aware of how grubby and disheveled he looked. Had to be something to do with the wedding, he figured. Maybe a sudden development, since neither Cassie nor Bonnie had mentioned this visit to him. For Cassie's sake, he hoped it wasn't anything serious, though knowing his daughter, she'd deal admirably with whatever it was.

He wondered if there was any way he could sneak into the house and get a quick shower before greeting Bonnie, who was sure to look as tidy and collected as always. At the very least, he'd like to wash his face and hands.

Carrying his gym bag in his left hand, he let himself into the kitchen and headed straight for the stairs. He didn't hear voices, but he assumed Cassie and Bonnie—maybe Kinley, too, if this was indeed a meeting about the wedding—were in the living room in the front of the house.

Walking softly so as not to draw attention to his arrival, he reached the top of the stairs and headed for his bedroom at the end of the hallway. He stopped in his tracks at the open doorway of the third bedroom, which Cassie had been using as a sewing room since she'd moved back in.

Too busy chatting to have heard his quiet arrival, Cassie and Bonnie stood in the cluttered bedroom, surrounded by fabric and garments, sewing machines, an iron and ironing board, a dressmaker's form and stacked boxes holding what he assumed to be other sewing supplies. An open sketchbook lay on the bed next to a tablet computer and a handful of colored pencils scattered across the duvet. He noted all those details from his peripheral vision, but his attention was focused solely on the center of the room, where Bonnie stood with her arms extended while Cassie focused on the measuring tape she'd wrapped around Bonnie's bustline. Paul was unable to resist looking in that direction, himself. For a small woman, Bonnie had a very nice shape—an observation that caused him to shift his weight uncomfortably and move his gym bag in front of him.

Perhaps it was that movement that drew Bonnie's attention in his direction. Seeing him standing there, she started and dropped her arms, dislodging the measuring tape. A wave of pink brightened her cheeks, though she managed a slightly abashed smile to greet him.

Looking around, Cassie said somewhat distractedly, "Oh, hi, Dad. I was just measuring Bonnie. You're home earlier than I expected."

"I decided to pass on the beer-and-pizza run after the match. Um, why were you measuring Bonnie?"

Making a notation on the sketch pad, Cassie replied without looking up. "I'm making a dress for her. It's an extra credit project for a class, and she very generously agreed to model for me. Didn't I mention it?"

"No, you didn't." For some reason, he suspected the omission had been deliberate, though he wasn't sure why she hadn't told him about the project. He glanced toward Bonnie, who was busily smoothing her fitted top over her floral skirt, seemingly giving the task much more attention than it warranted. "Hi."

Her hands stilled and she returned his smile, though he thought it looked just a bit strained. "Hi."

Was she embarrassed to have been caught in a somewhat awkward position? To assure her she shouldn't be, he kept his tone light when he said, "So Cassie roped you into being a dressmaker's dummy, huh? I won't tell you how many times she's draped fabric over me."

Bonnie's eyebrows rose. "I didn't know you made menswear, Cassie."

Paul sighed dramatically. "She doesn't."

That elicited Bonnie's musical laugh, as he'd hoped. She looked more comfortable now, her momentary discomfiture replaced by humor. Still scribbling in her sketchbook, Cassie ignored him pointedly.

Bonnie cocked her head and studied him more closely, as if suddenly noticing a few details. Now the one feeling at a disadvantage, he wished he'd had time for that face washing. "Did you forget your sunscreen?"

He wrinkled his nose automatically, feeling the tight, reddened skin pull with the movement. "I forgot to reapply it enough times during the kayaking trip yesterday. I wore some today for the soccer game," he added a bit defensively.

"Locking the barn after the horse got scorched," Cassie mumbled. Before he could ask her what the heck that was supposed to mean, she asked Bonnie, "Do you like this shape, Bonnie? It's a little different than what I've seen you wear, but I think it could be nice on you."

Taking his cue, Paul took a step back into the hallway. "If you'll excuse me, I need a quick shower."

"You need a long shower, Dad. Take your time."

Shooting a frown toward his grinning daughter, Paul turned and headed for his room, hoping Bonnie would still be around when he came out clean and freshly composed.

During her twenty-eight years, Bonnie had experienced sexual attraction before. Though she'd been focused for so long on her goal of running Bride Mountain Inn and had concentrated since her teen years on her career training, she'd dated in high school and had a semi-serious boyfriend in college, a couple of brief liaisons since. But until some ten minutes ago, she wasn't sure she'd ever been so utterly knocked out by a wave of throat-closing, heart-racing, nipple-tightening lust.

Just mentally picturing Paul's sudden appearance in that doorway—rumpled, grubby, sweaty, sunburned and virilely male to his sneakered toes—made her pulse trip again. She had to push the image firmly to the back of her mind to get through the remainder of her consultation with Cassie somewhat coherently, especially after she heard the shower running in another room. The fantasies that resulted from that sound were definitely going to have to wait until later, when she was alone.

She was quite impressed by Cassie's design skills as displayed by the sketches and garments Cassie showed her that she'd conceived and created. The wedding gown was ninety-nine percent completed, Cassie confided, but that was being kept under wraps till her wedding day. With the exception of Danielle, who'd helped her with a couple of the fittings, no one else had seen it yet, not even her parents.

"I'm sure it's beautiful," Bonnie said. "I can't wait to see you in it on your wedding day."

"I'm really happy with it. And I think Mike will like it."

"Well, that's all that matters, really, isn't it?" Bonnie had met Cassie's fiancé only once in passing when Cassie had brought him to see the inn last month on one of his brief trips home from London, where he had recently started his new job. He'd seemed very nice, in a clean-cut, boy-next-door way, and visibly eager for

Cassie to finish school, marry him and join him in England. "Will Mike be back in town before the wedding?"

Cassie sighed heavily. "No. In order to take off a couple of weeks for the honeymoon, he has to work right up until four days before the wedding. That's one reason I'm staying so busy, so I won't have time to miss him so much. Not that it works, really—but at least we get to talk by phone and computer every day."

She shook her head as if shaking off her momentary wistfulness and picked up the sketch pad again. "So, we're agreed on the leaf-green for the fabric?"

"It's a very pretty color." And also an expensive fabric, Bonnie fretted, having seen a swatch. Cassie had refused to even consider payment for the dress. She'd assured Bonnie that she'd collected a lot of fabric at clearance sales during the past few years and that she couldn't move it all with her to London. She was only sorry she didn't have time to make another garment from her sketched collection. She said she was partial to the skinny pants and beaded bolero, and she rather liked the formal-occasion gown, but just couldn't do either of them justice with the limited time she had. Having decided that the day-to-evening dress would be more functional for Bonnie, anyway, she'd chosen to focus on that.

Though of just over average height, Cassie seemed to have a knack for designing for a petite woman, Bonnie decided, studying the sketches again. They didn't look like regular-sized clothing simply cut shorter, but rather original designs intended to lengthen and slenderize while still emphasizing feminine curves. The sleek, sheath-style dress was a different shape from Bonnie's usual attire, but Cassie had assured her it was going to be incredibly flattering. What woman could resist that?

Cassie closed the sketchbook. "I have some peach tea in the fridge downstairs. Would you like a glass?"

Bonnie glanced at her watch. It was only a few minutes after four o'clock, and she wouldn't serve the Sunday evening sandwiches until six. Everything was ready to set out, so she didn't have to rush to the inn. "Yes, I'd love some, thank you. I have about an hour before I should head home."

She was not staying longer just to spend more time with Paul, she assured herself. Though that was certainly a perk.

She and Cassie sat at the kitchen table a few minutes later with their peach tea when Paul joined them. He was clean and groomed now, his hair damp but neatly combed, his jaw clean-shaven, his dirty sports clothes exchanged for a crisp blue cotton shirt and jeans. Seeing him now had the same impact as earlier, though she had herself under somewhat better control this time, having had a chance to prepare for his arrival.

"Well, don't you look spiffy," Cassie remarked, arching a brow as she glanced from her father to Bonnie and back again.

Paul gave his daughter a quizzical look. "Spiffy?" he repeated, passing her to reach into the refrigerator and pull out the tea pitcher.

She giggled. "Very."

He tugged lightly at her hair when he passed her to take a seat at the table, directly across from Bonnie. He met her eyes over the cookie jar centerpiece. "How did the fashion consultation go?"

"Your daughter is brilliant."

He winked. “Yes, I know. We try not to mention it in front of her, though. Gives her a big head.”

“Hey!” Cassie protested playfully. “I happen to be very modest about my genius.”

Paul groaned and Bonnie laughed, enjoying their affectionate interplay. Seeing them together gave her a wistful feeling, reminding her of her distant relationship with her own father. She would have loved to have been this close with him when she was younger. She’d often wondered if maybe she wouldn’t be so gun-shy about trusting in romantic promises if her dad had lived up to the ones he’d once made to her mom?

“How long have you been designing, Cassie?” she asked to distract herself from those regretful thoughts.

“Since I could hold a crayon. When I was little, I drew clothes for my paper dolls. Dad cut them out for me and made little tabs on them to fold over the dolls. I was too young to manipulate the scissors then.”

Bonnie glanced at Paul, who smiled sheepishly. “I told myself that scissors are tools, and tools are manly.”

“Then when I was a couple of years older,” Cassie went on, “I sketched outfits for my dolls and Grandma Bauer, my stepdad’s mother, helped me sew them. She was a professional seamstress when she was young. She helped me bring my sketches to life, taught me to sew, starting as soon as I was big enough to reach the foot pedal, which she put on a box for me.”

“Good woman,” Paul agreed. “Made the best pecan pie I ever put in my mouth. She passed away last year, sadly.”

“You really did have a supportive extended family, didn’t you?” Bonnie asked Cassie.

Cassie smiled over the rim of her glass. “I don’t remember Dad's parents, but Larry's family accepted me as their own and I've been able to see Mom's parents in North Carolina quite often. So, yeah, I hit the family jackpot. What about you? Do you have a large extended family? Are your parents and grandparents still living?"

"No, my grandparents are all gone. I have some aunts, uncles and cousins on my dad's side, but most of them live in Mississippi and Georgia and we don't see each other often." Running a finger through the condensation on the outside of her own glass, Bonnie added softly, "We lost our mother after a very brief illness almost four years ago. She had just turned fifty-eight."

Even after this much time, it was still hard to believe her mother was gone. And it still hurt every time she had to accept that it was true.

Paul reached across the table to lay a hand over hers. "I'm sorry."

"So am I," Cassie said, looking a bit stricken.

Bonnie spoke reassuringly, not wanting Cassie to feel badly about having asked the question. "It's okay."

"Never gets easier, does it?" Paul asked quietly.

Remembering he'd told her he'd lost his own parents young, she met his eyes, seeing the understanding there. "No," she said, "it doesn't."

He gave her fingers another little squeeze, then withdrew his hand, leaving her skin tingling in his wake.

"Is your father still living?" Cassie asked quietly.

Bonnie nodded. "My dad is still going strong. He travels all around the world, but he calls every so often and we see him occasionally. He says he thinks there must be Gypsy blood somewhere in the Carmichael background because he just can't seem to stay in one place for very long. He and my mom were married for ten years, but she simply couldn't pack up three kids and move every time the whim struck him. They divorced when I was only four. Mom raised us in Tennessee, but we came to visit Uncle Leo and Aunt Helen—and later just Uncle Leo—every summer and most holidays. Mom and Uncle Leo were very close, which was why he left the inn to my brother and sister and me. I, by the way, was his favorite."

Paul chuckled. "That doesn't surprise me."

"Why were you his favorite?" Cassie asked, wide-eyed.

"Because I was the one most obsessed with someday reopening and running the inn," Bonnie explained, rather relieved that neither had focused on her unusual relationship with her father. Maybe they'd been able to tell by the way she'd glossed over the subject so quickly that it wasn't something she liked to discuss. To be honest, she had nothing else to say about it just then. She didn't even remember a time when her father had been a permanent part of her life. "You know how you made clothes for your dolls? When I was little, I played innkeeper with all my dolls and stuffed animals. I charged my sister a nickel a night to let her dolls stay in the cardboard hotel rooms I created."

Cassie laughed. "Really? That's hilarious. Did she pay?"

"Of course. I convinced her that only the coolest dolls stayed in my hotel. Kinley's always been a bit competitive."

Grinning, Paul said, "And I thought Kinley was the salesperson in the family."

"Oh, she is. Kinley could sell sand in a desert."

"And you?"

"I can turn that desert into an inviting place to stay," she quipped.

"Or to have a wedding," Cassie suggested.

"That, too."

Cassie glanced at the clock on the yellow wall of her dad's cheery, stainless-and-slate kitchen. "Oops. I have to cut out. I promised Jenna I'd take her and a couple of her friends to a movie tonight. Jenna used the old 'spending as much time with my sister as I can' spiel, but really she just needed a chauffeur who won't get exasperated with them for acting goofy in the car."

Bonnie started to rise. "I should go, too."

"Oh, no, finish your tea. You said you don't have to leave until five or so, right? You can give Dad some more cooking tips." Cassie's grin included both of them. "It would be a shame for him to have gotten all spiffed up for nothing."

She planted a kiss on her father's cheek, then whirled out of the room without giving either of them much time to do more than wave goodbye.

"My daughter," Paul said wryly, "has all the subtlety of a steamroller. If you have to get back to the inn…"

After only a momentary hesitation, she picked up her drinking glass again. "I'm not in that much of a hurry."

His approving smile was warm enough to make her need a sip of the chilled beverage to clear her head. She felt the icy liquid slide down her throat, but it did little to cool her. The heat Paul's gaze ignited inside her could not be assuaged with any amount of iced tea.

"It was a nice surprise finding you here today," he said. "A *very* nice surprise."

Okay, flirting again. She still remembered how to do that. Or so she hoped. "I have to admit I hoped you'd show up this afternoon."

He reached into the cookie jar and drew out a cookie. "Cranberry-oatmeal," he said, showing it to her. "Cassie made them. Would you like one?"

"No, thank you." They did look good, though, she mused, making a mental note to prepare some for her guests soon. Always working, she chided herself then, thinking of how often she'd accused her sister of the same thing. She really should focus on this rare break from the inn, especially with such charming company. "So, you played soccer today?"

"Yeah. Couple of guys I kayaked with yesterday asked if I wanted to fill in for someone who couldn't play today. It'd been a while since I played, but I remembered the basics. Scored a goal."

She couldn't help but smile in response to his obvious pride. "Congratulations."

"Thanks. My team still lost, but that was one more point in our favor."

"How's the leg?"

"The, uh—?"

"I saw the blood."

"Oh." He grimaced ruefully. "It's fine. Just a scratch. Got tackled by a big, burly guy twice my size."

Something about the way he said that made her suspect it was completely fabricated—and that he wasn't really trying to convince her otherwise. She smiled. "Is that right?"

"Huge," he reiterated with a grin around his cookie.

"It's a wonder you survived," she said gravely.

"What can I say? I'm a tough guy."

The sound that escaped her sounded disconcertingly like a giggle. She drained her tea glass.

"Can I get you a refill?" Paul offered.

"No, thank you. I really do have to head back to the inn soon for dinner service. I don't want to keep the guests waiting."

She stood to carry her glass to the sink. When she turned, she found that Paul had followed her. He set his glass beside hers, then smiled down at her. "It was a nice surprise to find you here. I thought I'd have to wait until tomorrow to see you."

"Cassie called yesterday to arrange this. I thought she had mentioned it to you."

"No. But then I haven't seen her much the past few days. Her schedule is pretty hectic at the moment, and she just keeps adding things to do."

"She said staying busy keeps her from obsessing about the wedding."

Paul shrugged. "She's happiest when she's going a thousand miles an hour. Always has been. Holly and I used to say if we could bottle Cassie's energy and sell it, we could both retire young."

Bonnie lifted a hand to brush her fingertips lightly over his reddened cheek. "Did you put anything on this?"

"Cassie gave me some kind of moisturizing lotion—along with a lengthy lecture about taking better care of my skin. It isn't as bad as it looks. I just got careless, I guess."

She made a face. "I can burn just walking from the

car to the house. I have to slather on sunscreen every day."

Mimicking her gesture, he slid his hand across her cheek, his gaze following the movement. "You have such fair skin. It's lovely."

She'd have thought she'd be getting more accustomed to him by now, but every touch, every shared glance still felt so new. So exhilarating.

Considering they had acknowledged their mutual attraction only the day before, and that she still wasn't sure Paul was interested in anything more than a fling, she wasn't sure it was at all wise to be falling this hard for him. She would prefer to keep her well-guarded heart unbroken, whatever happened with Paul.

"You look so serious all of a sudden." The way he studied her face made her wonder just how long she'd been standing there gazing up at him.

She forced a smile. "Sorry. A lot on my mind, I guess."

His thumb slid slowly across her lower lip. His gaze followed the movement. "I don't mean to add to your stress level. I'd much rather you see me as someone to relax and have some fun with."

Tempting words. She had no doubt that she and Paul could have quite a bit of fun together.

"I'd like that," she said.

His mouth was very close to hers when he murmured, "So would I."

He seemed to be leaving the next move up to her, and she appreciated that. And because she liked him so very much, she made that move, leaning into him and lifting her face to his.

His mouth closed over hers, eagerly but not hurriedly. He took his time with that first kiss—almost as if relishing every second of anticipation. Her eyelids drifted close, allowing her to savor the feel, the taste, the fresh-showered scent of him. She had noted his strength when he'd lifted her down from the stepladder two days ago. Being pressed full-length against him, she felt again the well-developed muscles that testified to his active lifestyle. Despite their height difference, they fit together quite well, with her tucked snugly into his arms, him wrapped warmly around her.

Standing on tiptoe, she slid her arms around his neck. The kiss deepened as he slipped his tongue between her welcoming lips for a more intimate exploration. Her heart raced and every inch of her body felt tight, tingly. For a first kiss from this sexy schoolteacher, she would grade this one an A plus.

"I've wanted to do that since I picked you up off the floor that first day at the inn," Paul confessed with a slightly unsteady grin.

"You did manage to knock me off my feet the first time we met," she murmured and pressed another quick kiss to his smiling lips.

Somewhat reluctantly, she allowed her arms to drop from around his neck, automatically smoothing the raised hem of her top over her skirt. "As much as I hate to leave, I really do have to get back to work."

"I wish you could stay longer, but I understand. I'll see you tomorrow?"

"Absolutely. I have some things to do in the morning, but I'm free after noon. I've made arrangements for Rhoda and Kinley to take over some of my duties so I can have a day off."

"So what would you like to do on your day off? Playtime or pampering? Jeans or dress up?"

She didn't even have to think about her answer. "Play," she said. "I've been busy indoors cooking and cleaning and hosting for the past few weeks. Unless you've had enough outdoor fun lately?"

He grinned, and his still-reddened nose crinkled appealingly. "You should know by now that I'm going to head outside any chance I get."

"I'm getting that idea."

"Who do you think suggested Cassie have an outdoor wedding?"

"So you get the blame if it rains."

"Oh, no, we'll still blame you for that," he assured her, tongue in cheek.

Feigning indignation, she shook a finger at him. "Oh, thanks so much."

"Just kidding," he assured her, laughing. "I have a buddy who owns a trail-ride operation about an hour's drive from the inn. He offers buggy rides, too. Do either of those things appeal to you?"

"I would love to go on a trail ride," she said eagerly. "Kinley and I used to take rides with friends in the Smoky Mountains when we lived in Tennessee, but I haven't been on horseback since we moved to Virginia. I've missed it."

There were so many things she hadn't taken time to do while she'd been busy with the inn, she thought with a slight shake of her head. It was definitely time to remedy that.

Paul nodded approvingly. "I'll call Tim, my friend, and let him know we'll be there tomorrow afternoon. I'll pick you up at one?"

"I'll look forward to it."

He brushed another kiss across her lips and murmured, "So will I."

Considering the heady emotions she felt when she headed back to the inn, it wouldn't surprise her at all if tomorrow's outdoor activities led to eventual—perhaps sooner rather than later—indoor pursuits.

After a satisfactory meeting the next morning with two women who wanted to reserve the inn for an upcoming class reunion, Bonnie and Kinley exchanged their customary high five to celebrate another successful booking. "That will be a fun group," Kinley predicted.

"I think you're right."

"Now, isn't it time for you to change for your date?" Kinley looked pointedly at her watch.

Bonnie wrinkled her nose at the unnecessary reminder. "Yes, I'm going. You'll check on the guests later if I'm not back by game time?"

"Of course. Dan and I are having an early dinner at the café tonight, then we'll come back here for board games in the parlor with the guests. Stay out as long as you want. You've earned some time off. You've worked half a day, anyway."

"Okay, then. I'll have my phone if you need me, of course."

Kinley rolled her eyes dramatically. "I think we can get by without you for a few hours, Bon. Heck, stay out all night. You deserve that every once in a while, too."

"I'm not staying out all night," Bonnie muttered. At least, that wasn't in her plans at the moment.

"So, just what is going on with you and Paul, hmm?"

"Well, I'm not changing my Facebook status to 'in a relationship,'" Bonnie retorted, then sighed. "We're going to spend a few hours together today, okay? A trail-ride date. I like him, he likes me. Maybe it will lead somewhere, maybe it won't, but it's no big deal right now, all right?"

"Sorry, little sis, I'm only teasing. I think it's great that you're getting out. You spend too much time here at the inn. You need to have a life outside of work. Paul seems like a nice guy, probably fun to hang out with. Though, ah—?"

Bonnie felt her left eyebrow shoot upward. "What?"

"Well, just be careful. I mean, yeah, he seems great, but a good-looking guy his age who's still single..." Kinley shrugged. "Could be a bit of a player, you know? Just keep that at the back of your mind while you're having a good time with him."

Was Kinley seriously turning maternal on her? Only three years separated them, and Kinley wasn't usually one to take her "big sister" status all that seriously. So why now?

"Like I said," she repeated slowly. "We're just having fun, seeing what happens."

"As long as what happens isn't you getting hurt by mixed messages or unrealistic expectations," Kinley said quietly. "Trust me, that's not fun."

Bonnie was aware that divorced Kinley spoke from painful experience. Her youthful marriage had ended in disappointment and some humiliation when her husband of only months had abruptly changed his mind about wanting to be married. Holding her head up proudly, Kinley had thrown herself into work, becoming more of a perfectionist than ever, but Bonnie knew how deeply the failed marriage had hurt her sister. After their father's abandonment and her husband's betrayal, it had been hard for Kinley to trust her feelings for Dan at first, though it hadn't taken him long to win her heart.

"I'm not letting my expectations get too high," she promised. "You don't need to worry about me—but thanks for caring."

Her sister laughed with sudden self-consciousness and tucked a strand of hair behind her right ear. "I guess I was channeling Mom there for a minute. Forget what I said. Go have fun with the hunky teacher. The inn will be safely in one piece when you get back."

"I'd appreciate that. Call if you—"

"Yes, I know. Go."

Leaving Kinley with her computer work and phone calls in the small, tidy office, Bonnie headed down to her apartment to prepare for Paul's arrival. She changed into a pair of jeans and a cap-sleeved yellow eyelet blouse over a matching lace-trimmed tank top, then eyed her reflection critically. She had aimed for cute and casual, and she decided she'd hit the mark closely enough. She stashed a ponytail band in her pocket in case she needed her hair out of the way later.

She had to climb on a stool to reach the box on a top shelf in her walk-in closet that held the boots she'd worn for horseback riding in the past. It had been so long since she'd worn them that she had to wipe off the dust before she put them on. They weren't Western-style boots, but rather a low-heeled brown leather ankle boot with a slender toe box that made them work well enough in stirrups. Stuffing her phone and a few other necessities into a small, cross-body bag that would leave her hands free, she pronounced herself as prepared as possible.

She checked the time. Great. She was ready twenty minutes early, which gave her time to get nervous about the outing for no good reason. To distract herself, she headed back out of her apartment. She would wait for Paul outside.

She was sitting on the front porch in a rocking chair, chatting with a couple of their guests, when she spotted Paul's car coming up the road. In deference to the nice weather thus far that day, he'd left the top down on his yellow Mustang, making her glad she'd thought to bring the hair band.

"Wowza. Hottie in a convertible alert," one of the guests, Linda Dougherty, commented from the chair closest to Bonnie's.

Her husband, Andy, grumbled from her other side, "I am still here, you know."

"Why, yes, you are," Linda shot back at him with a bright smile. "And weren't you the one who mentioned just yesterday that you think the owner of Bride Mountain Café is a knockout?"

He chuckled, sounding unabashed. "I might have noticed in passing."

"I thought so."

Smiling at their byplay, Bonnie stood. "If you'll excuse me, that's my ride."

"Lucky you," Linda said.

Andy made a show of looking at his watch. "Maybe we should head down to the café. I'm in the mood for a big slice of pie."

He grunted when his wife punched him on the arm.

Paul tugged off his sunglasses to greet Bonnie with

a big smile. His short-sleeve knit shirt and nicely fitted jeans highlighted his excellent physical condition. He, too, wore boots, though she noted at once that his were traditionally Western-styled, and looked well used. They suited him, but then she hadn't seen him in anything yet that didn't look good on him.

He leaned down to brush a light kiss against her cheek as he reached to open the passenger side door. "You look very nice."

"Thank you."

He waited until she was seated, then closed her door. "I can put the top up, if you prefer."

"Oh, no, leave it down. It's been years since I rode in a convertible."

He seemed pleased by her choice. As he climbed behind the wheel and slid his sunglasses back onto his nose, she pulled back her hair, securing it in a high ponytail. She put on her sunglasses and fastened her seat belt.

Paul shot a smile her way. "Ready?"

Lifting her chin, she replied boldly, "Ready."

Grinning, he started the engine. Bonnie waved to her watching guests as they drove away from the inn, her ponytail swinging in the warm breeze.

She enjoyed feeling the wind against her cheeks as Paul drove into the mountains on winding, rising roads that offered spectacular views around each turn. She would have been content just to savor the ride, but she suspected Paul looked forward to their other plans. As if in confirmation, he spoke over the noise of the road, wind and engine. "So, you like horses?"

"I love them," she answered candidly. "I never had one of my own, but my high school boyfriend lived on a ranch where they raised Tennessee Walkers. We rode almost every weekend until he dumped me for the local rodeo queen."

Though she'd hoped to elicit a chuckle from him with her ironic comment, he frowned for a moment. "Sounds like a jerk."

She laughed. "He was. To be honest, I liked his horses better than I liked him. I'm really looking forward to this ride."

His smile had returned when he looked away from the road just long enough to slant a quick glance at her. "Great. Think of your trail rides with your sister when we mount up, not your old boyfriend, will you? Or better yet, just focus on me."

Even though she knew he was teasing, she nodded with mock gravity. "I think I can do that."

As if she had any choice.

Chapter Five

It really was a wonder, Paul thought a couple of hours later, that he hadn't crashed his car right off a cliff. Okay, so maybe that was an exaggeration, since he'd been fully in control of the vehicle, but he couldn't deny that too much of his attention had been zeroed in on Bonnie.

She always looked pretty but today, in her curve-hugging jeans and lace blouse over a low-scooped, lace-trimmed tank, with little curls escaping her loose ponytail and her face flushed by wind and sun, she was utterly irresistible.

Tim Snow, Paul's friend who co-owned the business alliteratively named Blue Ridge Backtrails, raised both eyebrows when he watched Bonnie bonding sweetly with a saddled bay Tennessee Walker gelding. Bonnie was nose to nose with the horse, who looked as charmed by her as Paul felt. She seemed oblivious to the fact that the horse towered over her, and showed no fear when it blew a breath out its nostrils, then nuzzled her hard enough to make her wobble a bit on her feet. Bonnie merely laughed and reached up to rub the horse's eagerly cocked ears. The sun washed over them both, bringing out the red in the Walker's coat and the gold in Bonnie's blond hair.

"Whoa," Tim, who was two or three years younger than Paul, said beneath his breath. "Now that is a pretty sight."

Hands in the pockets of his jeans, Paul kept his gaze on Bonnie and her new pal. "Agreed."

"Friend of your daughter's?"

Paul's smile faded into a scowl. "Friend of *mine*."

"Dude. Seriously? I mean, sorry about the question, but, uh…"

Reminding himself that Bonnie looked deceptively younger with her hair in the ponytail and her lace top and jeans, Paul changed the subject abruptly. "So, are you riding with us?"

"Well, I can if you want me to, since I don't have any other rides booked until later today, but you know the trail well enough to take her out yourself, if you prefer." Tim wiggled his eyebrows just enough to make it clear what he would do in Paul's boots.

Tim was a natural entertainer as a trail ride guide, with an endless supply of jokes and quips and stories. Yet as much as Paul enjoyed those rides with his friend, he liked the idea of leaving him behind today. "I'll take her, then. I'm sure you have things to do here."

His brown eyes glinting with humor, Tim nodded. "I do have some calls to make."

Paul turned toward Bonnie. "So, is that the mount you like?"

Planting a noisy kiss just above the bay's nose, Bonnie then turned a beaming smile toward Paul. His gut tightened in response.

"If he follows me home, can I keep him?" she asked with a laugh.

He cleared his throat and spoke as lightly as she had. "Well, if your brother can keep a big dog, you should be able to have a pet horse."

"That's Stewie, ma'am, and he's a marshmallow when it comes to pretty ladies who fawn over him," Tim informed her in a drawl, sauntering over in her direction. "Paul, are you riding Ace?"

"Of course." Paul had already moved toward the black Walker who stood quietly near the water trough in the spacious corral among a group of saddled horses who watched Paul approach with idle curiosity.

"Hey, Ace, how's it going?"

He wasn't sure if his favorite mount remembered him specifically, but Ace responded to his voice with a friendly nicker and head nod. After greeting the horse with pats, he mounted, sliding his left boot into the left stirrup and swinging his right leg over easily. He saw that Tim had Bonnie settled comfortably in Stewie's saddle, the stirrups adjusted for her shorter legs.

Holding Ace's reins loosely in his right hand, he nudged the horse forward toward Bonnie and Stewie. "Ready?"

She was beaming so brightly that he couldn't help mentally patting himself on the back for coming up with this idea, even if belatedly. "Absolutely," she assured him.

"You kids have fun," Tim said with a grin, stepping back out of the way. "You've got my number if you get into trouble, Paul."

Looking at Bonnie sitting so happily on the eager bay, her bright eyes glittering like blue diamonds before she hid them behind her sunglasses again, Paul figured he was already in trouble. But there was nothing Tim could do to help him.

They couldn't have asked for a nicer day for the ride. It was warm, but not uncomfortably so, with a nice breeze to ruffle their hair and cool their skin. A few clouds dotted the sky, diffusing the sunlight when they weren't beneath the shade of the lush trees lining the trail. Off in the distance beyond the mountain peaks they could see a heavier bank of clouds gathering for the rain predicted that evening, but Bonnie figured they had several hours yet to enjoy being outdoors.

Because he knew the way, Paul rode lead with Bonnie following on Stewie. Paul kept the pace slow, and the horses plodded easily over the very familiar trail. The only sounds other than the steady clops of hooves were the birds singing overhead and the breeze rustling leaves, underscored occasionally by running water sounds from the shallow streams that crisscrossed the woods. She and Paul were able to chat easily enough without raising their voices to disturb the peace of their surroundings.

"It was nice of your friend to let us take the horses by ourselves," she commented. "The trail ride operation Kinley and I used back in Tennessee never let anyone go out without a guide, even experienced horsemen. It was against their policy."

"I've ridden this trail with Cassie and/or the twins and their friends almost too many times to count," Paul explained. "I've been friends with Tim for years, so he knows he can trust me to take care of the horses—and you. Cassie and I went along on his first guided ride when he and his partner, Jase, opened their business a few years back. Now they're a big success. In addition to the trail and buggy rides, they provide hunting and fishing guides in seasons. A general-purpose outfitting operation, you could say."

She admired the sight of Paul sitting so comfortably astride the black horse. She didn't mind at all following him on the trail, as it allowed her to appreciate him without being overly obvious about it. "Did you grow up around horses?"

He shook his head, looking over his shoulder to answer. "I grew up in Raleigh, North Carolina. My parents were both in their early forties when I came along to surprise them, and I was only a toddler when my dad was diagnosed with multiple sclerosis. He wasn't able to get out and do much, and Mom spent most of her time either working or taking care of Dad. I think she pretty much wore herself out before we lost him, which was why she wasn't able to fight off the infection that killed her only a few years later. I did all I could to help her, but she insisted on doing most of it herself. I mean, I got plenty of attention from them, don't get me wrong. We were all close, and I miss them both, but we didn't do a lot of outdoor stuff like horseback riding."

She suspected from his tone that he didn't want an expression of sympathy just then. The day was too nice to be spoiled by sadness. Instead she asked, "How did you end up being such a jock and a horseman?"

He chuckled, and he seemed pleased that she'd lightened the conversation. "My mom's younger brother, my uncle Brian, made a point to take me out and do 'manly stuff' like hunting and fishing and sports at least once a month. Great guy. We're still close, though we don't get to see each other as often as we'd like. I like sports and kayaking and other outdoor pursuits, but I'd hardly call myself a jock. I have a master's degree in mathematics, which some people consider pretty much the opposite of jock-hood."

Bonnie laughed, conceding his point.

"As for horses, Cassie developed a love of horses when she was a kid and she begged me to take her riding. I pretty much learned with her. Needless to say, Larry's not much of a rider and Holly is afraid of horses, so riding outings fell to me."

Stewie lowered his head to investigate a clump of grass, but cooperated when she tightened the reins enough to keep him on the trail. She reached down to pat him absently on the neck, thinking about the things Paul had said. Hearing about his childhood explained a few things—like why he was so generous with his time, so unselfish in helping Holly and Larry not only with his own daughter but with their twins, as his uncle had done for him. He'd grown up helping out at home, which had made him self-sufficient, handy around the house and accustomed to taking care of others. But maybe this explained, as well, why he rather looked forward to his "empty nest"?

"You said you're from North Carolina? Holly, too, I suppose, since you dated in high school?"

He waited until Ace negotiated a sharp rise in the rocky trail and Bonnie had safely followed before answering. "Yeah, we both grew up in Raleigh. Holly and Larry came to Virginia when he accepted an engineering position with Tech. After visiting them here and liking the area, I decided to settle here, myself, to be closer to Cassie. She was nine then."

Another narrow creek crossed the path, and Ace lowered his head to the water. Paul didn't urge the horse on, grinning around at Bonnie instead. "Before you ask, I have no plans to move to London. Or to Dallas."

Holding Stewie's reins loosely while he shifted his weight, but remained quietly in place, Bonnie lifted an eyebrow in question. "Dallas?"

"Oh, I guess you haven't heard. Holly and Larry and the twins are moving to Texas after the wedding. Holly's taking a position in a law firm there, and Larry's already found another faculty job. They'll be back and forth to Dallas between now and then making arrangements, though of course they'll be here for all the wedding festivities."

"No, I didn't know. Wow. How do you feel about that?" Was it a relief to know he wouldn't be called on frequently to chauffeur or chaperone after that move? She couldn't say she would blame him for looking forward to not being always on standby, to having no one to look out for but himself for the first time since he was just a boy. Or would he miss them as much as she knew he'd miss Cassie? Would he miss Holly?

Rather than answering, he raised himself in the stirrups and swung his right leg backward, dismounting in one fluid movement. It was a pretty spot for a break, shaded by tall trees between which she could see a spreading vista of hills and valleys and the ridge of blue-tinted mountains against the clouded horizon.

Something splashed in the rippling creek—fish? turtle?—and a cardinal flashed red as it darted from one tree to another. She'd grown up in the foothills of the Tennessee Smoky Mountains and had spent a significant part of her youth here in the Blue Ridge Highlands. She couldn't imagine living anywhere that didn't have a view like this within an hour's drive. Not to mention the view from the back porch of Bride Mountain Inn.

Dropping Ace's reins straight down to the ground and saying, "Stand," Paul then walked over to reach up to Bonnie. "Want to walk around a bit?"

Though she could have dismounted easily enough, she allowed him to assist her down, just for the chance to feel his hands on her again. He didn't immediately release her when her feet were on the ground, leaving his hands loosely at her waist. He spoke to Stewie as he let the reins drop. "Stand."

"We don't need to tie them?"

Smiling down at her, he shook his head. "These are Tim's two best-trained trail horses. They'll stay ground tied for a short break."

"They're both beautiful horses. It's easy to tell they're well cared for."

"They're treated like royalty," he agreed with a chuckle. "Tim and Jase are pretty strict with their trail riders. They make sure the horses are treated right."

Which was only further testament to how much Tim trusted Paul, she thought. "How long have you known them?"

"I met Tim a few months after I moved to Virginia a dozen years ago. Actually, I dated his sister for a short time," he confessed. "Laura and I drifted apart, but I stayed friends with her brother—and with her, for that matter. She ended up marrying Tim's partner, Jase. Funny story, she always said she couldn't stand the guy, but after Jase got badly hurt in a rodeo accident, she realized she'd been mistaken. She spent time with him while he recuperated, and a few months later they were engaged."

The genuine amusement in Paul's voice let her know he had no lingering feelings for Laura, but she noted he'd still not answered her question about Holly moving away. She stepped away from him, casually dislodging his hands, and moved to the water's edge, smiling when she saw two turtles sunning themselves on a big rock. Neither showed any reciprocal interest in her as they soaked in the warmth.

"I'm still processing the way I feel about it," Paul said quietly from behind her.

She looked over her shoulder in question. "What?"

His fingertips in his pockets, he met her gaze with a funny little smile she couldn't quite interpret. "You asked how I felt about the Bauer family moving away. I'm still getting used to the idea. I'm happy for Holly, of course. She's worked hard for a career opportunity like this. But it's going to seem strange being here with everyone else spread so far apart."

She bent to pick up a pretty little gray rock, smoothed by years of tumbling in the stream. "I'm sure there's a need for math teachers in Texas."

"Dallas is Holly's path now, not mine. We'll always be connected by Cassie, maybe some grandkids someday—but now it's time for us to go our own ways. I'm just trying to decide what my way is now. Got a whole world of options open to me."

She bit her lip in response to that breezy comment. After a moment's mental debate, she had to ask. "Are you sorry? That you and Holly didn't stay together, I mean?"

He laughed then, somewhat incredulously. "No, of course not. Holly and I were just kids when we were together, not the same people we are today at all. Even if we had tried to stay together for Cassie's sake, it wouldn't have lasted. Our goals and ambitions were completely different. We'd have driven each other crazy before too long. She and Larry were pretty much made for each other, and you couldn't find a happier family if you tried."

Bonnie looked at the sleepy turtles again. She wondered if part of the difference between Paul and Holly had been that she had wanted marriage and several children, whereas he had liked living on his own for the most part. But she really should stop trying to analyze Paul and simply enjoy this outing with him.

Stewie snorted and tossed his head, then nuzzled a tasty-looking plant at his feet. Bonnie chuckled. "I think he's reminding us that we have more trail to ride."

"He can wait another minute."

She hadn't been aware that Paul had moved until she felt his hands on her shoulders. She turned with a smile and lifted her face to him even as his mouth descended toward hers. Wrapping her arms around his neck, she decided the horses could wait a bit longer than a minute.

He took his time kissing her, apparently in no hurry to return to the ride. In this pretty spot with the music of nature serenading her and Paul's arms warm around her, she could think of no reason at all to rush back to reality. She closed her eyes and savored every sound, every sensation, every inch of his body pressed to hers.

Her heavy lids rose again when eventually he separated their lips, though he kept his face close to hers. Their gazes locked and a slow smile tilted the corners of his mouth. "I've been wanting to do that ever since I picked you up this afternoon," he confessed.

She smiled at him. "I'm glad you finally got around to it."

He chuckled and brushed another light kiss over her upwardly curved lips. "You look really good on horseback. But then, you always look good."

"And you are quite the smooth talker," she replied, running a fingertip along his firm jawline. "But I'm not complaining."

"I'm only speaking the truth," he assured her. "Tim thinks I'm a lucky guy to have you here with me today. And I agree."

Stewie flicked his tail and shifted his weight again, dislodging a little avalanche of pebbles. One of the turtles splashed noisily from the rock into the water, and Ace shook his head, perhaps shooing a fly, his tack rattling. Those sounds drew Bonnie's attention, making her aware that the afternoon was rushing by. Paul sighed as if in silent acknowledgment.

"I guess we'd better mount up," he said. "Come on, I'll help you up."

With one last lingering glance around the magical little glen, she turned and walked to her waiting horse.

The cloud cover had grown thicker by the time they eventually returned to the stables, so that it looked later in the day than it actually was. Bonnie could almost smell a hint of the approaching rain in the air. They needed rain for the gardens back at the inn, but she was always relieved when showers fell early in the week rather than weekends when weddings or other outdoor events were usually scheduled.

She kissed Stewie's velvety nose and thanked him for being such an obliging mount for the pleasant ride. Stewie nodded and chuffed, which she decided to interpret as, "You're welcome."

"It was nice to meet you, Bonnie." Tim tugged the brim of his Western-style hat in a charmingly old-fashioned gesture. "You come back anytime, you hear?"

She promised him she would recommend his services to future guests of the inn now that she had checked out the business for herself. It was just over an hour's drive from the inn, and she could assure anyone interested that it was an outing well worth the time and cost—though she noted that Tim refused to accept payment from Paul when it was offered.

Just in case the rain began sooner than expected, Paul put the top up on his car before driving out of the lot. Only ten minutes or so into the drive, he cleared his throat. "I know it's a bit too early for dinner, but I'm hungry. How do you feel about stopping for a snack?"

She glanced at her watch. Though it was only a quarter till five, she was a little hungry, too. Maybe due to the ride, the fresh air or just the power of suggestion, but whatever the reason, she agreed. "I could eat."

"There's a pretty decent diner about five miles on down the road. The kids like to stop there for burgers or pie after a ride."

"Sounds good."

He nodded without looking away from the road.

The section they were on was steep and winding with occasional drops off the sides beyond narrow gravel shoulders, requiring all his attention. It was beautiful countryside but a drive that called for caution, and she was pleased that he took their safety seriously. Unlike some reckless drivers, she thought with a disapproving shake of her head as two young people on a motorcycle, guy driving, girl clinging to his waist, buzzed around them from behind. They looked to be in their late teens or early twenties and appeared to be laughing because they'd passed the older driver in the yellow sport coupe. At least they were wearing helmets, though their shorts and T-shirts would do little to protect them in a fall.

"Moron," Paul muttered, watching as the bike leaned almost sideways to disappear around the next sharp curve ahead. "If I saw anyone driving like that with my daughter on the back, I'd—uh..."

He grimaced. "Okay, maybe that sounded a little curmudgeonly."

She shrugged. "I totally agree. He's being reckless. I hope they don't—"

Paul rounded the corner just in time to see the motorcycle wobble, fishtail, then skid over the edge of the road and out of sight.

Chapter Six

Paul slammed on the brakes and pulled his car to the side of the road. "Call 911," he said, even as he turned on the emergency flashers and all but leaped out of the driver's seat.

Bonnie scrambled after him, the phone already at her ear. Reaching the side of the road where the bike had gone over, Paul hesitated only long enough to look down through the broken and flattened brush at the top of the hillside that fell from the roadway. "Tell them to send an ambulance," he said before disappearing into the matted foliage.

She was almost afraid of what she might see when she looked over after him once she'd been assured help was on the way. The hill wasn't as steep as it had at first appeared, though the bike had still tumbled a good way down from the road. It lay in a crumpled heap against a tree. The riders had been thrown clear. She could see that the driver had tugged off his helmet and was struggling to sit up. Paul knelt beside the woman, who sprawled awkwardly on her back, her helmet still in place.

Bonnie slipped and stumbled as she made her way down to the others, but remained on her feet. "You should lie back down," she said to the young man, who swayed as he struggled to rise. She rested a hand on his shoulder, wincing at the sight of his scraped and bleeding arms and legs. His right foot seemed to be twisted at an odd angle and she suspected his ankle was broken. She worried that there could be other injuries not as immediately apparent. "Just lie still. An ambulance is on the way."

He turned his face to her, his dark eyes wide with shock and pain. His sandy hair was matted to his head, and his face had gone pale beneath his tan. The helmet and face shield had protected his head, but she had no way of knowing if he had neck or spine injuries. "My girlfriend," he mumbled. "Cheryl…"

"My friend is taking care of her," she said firmly, nudging him back down to the rocky ground. "What's your name?"

He shifted uncomfortably and drew a ragged breath. She suspected the numbness from the initial shock was wearing off, and that the pain would worsen rapidly. "Kyle. Kyle Neighbors."

"Okay, Kyle. Lie down and I'll check on your friend."

His breathing was a series of low moans now, but he managed a nod with his eyes squeezed shut, his hands fisted into the grass at his sides. Bonnie scooted over to Paul. "How is she?"

"She has some injuries, but she's going to be fine," he said bracingly, the words as much for Cheryl as for Bonnie.

He'd lifted the face shield on the helmet to reveal Cheryl's pale, tear-streaked face. Wild red curls fell from beneath the helmet, lying in a tangled mass beneath her on the ground. She cried softly, a mixture of sobs and low moans.

Bonnie saw that Paul had one hand pressed against Cheryl's upper leg. Blood oozed from beneath his fingers, making her aware that he was putting pressure on a wound to slow the bleeding. Without stopping to think, she tugged off her eyelet shirt, leaving her clad in the lace-trimmed tank top. "Here. Use this as a bandage or tourniquet," she offered, extending the shirt to Paul. "Whatever you need."

"It'll be ruined."

"Doesn't matter." She caught the injured woman's flailing arm. "Cheryl, my name is Bonnie. Lie still, okay? Help is coming."

"Helmet… Take it off."

"Let's leave it on for now," Paul said gently. "We don't know if there are any spinal injuries."

As her initial daze from the accident wore off, Cheryl became more agitated, squirming and crying out from pain and fear. Still putting pressure on the bleeding wound, now using Bonnie's shirt as a pad, Paul finally spoke firmly to the young woman, in what Bonnie imagined to be his father and schoolteacher voice.

"Cheryl, you're going to have to be still now," he ordered, his tone kind but implacable. "I know you're scared and you're in a lot of pain, but you have to be brave until the ambulance gets here, or you're going to make everything much worse. Do you understand?"

Subsiding into quiet tears, Cheryl nodded as best she could in the helmet.

Bonnie couldn't help but be impressed by the way Paul had taken charge of the scene. He was so different now than the easygoing horseman who'd flirted with her on the trail, the sunburned athlete who'd kissed her in his kitchen. This, she realized, was the man everyone called upon in a crisis, and now she had a better understanding of why.

"But it hurts," Cheryl whispered on a sob.

His firm tone immediately softening, Paul rested a hand comfortingly on the young woman's shoulder. "I know," he said, "and help is on the way. We're going to take very good care of you until it arrives, okay?"

Biting her lip, Cheryl nodded again, her eyes fixed on Paul's face as if she drew strength from his confidence and kindness. And here, Bonnie thought, was the special side of him that made so many people love him. She was all too close to that point, herself.

"Where's Kyle?" Cheryl asked, seeming to suddenly think a bit more clearly through her pain and disorientation.

"Kyle's fine," Bonnie assured her. "If you'll be as calm as you can for Paul, I'll go check on him again."

"O-okay."

Bonnie patted the younger woman's shoulder bracingly and moved to Kyle, who lay in the same position as she'd left him, moaning and occasionally cursing beneath his breath. Seeing the tears streaking his cheeks, she rested her hand on his shoulder. "I'm sorry you're hurting. The ambulance should be here soon."

She heard occasional traffic pass above, but no one stopped. There weren't many cars on the road on a Monday midafternoon. She knew they weren't visible to the people passing; all they would see was Paul's car parked on the shoulder with the hazard lights flashing, as if he'd run out of gas or had engine trouble. She couldn't help wondering how long Kyle and Cheryl would have lain here if she and Paul hadn't witnessed the accident.

A drop of water fell on her hand, and for a moment she thought it was one of Kyle's tears. But then more followed and she realized it was beginning to rain, very lightly at the moment but sure to strengthen. She hoped the heavy rain would hold off just a little longer, for all of their sakes.

"Oh, thank God," she murmured only a moment later, finally hearing the muted wail of an approaching siren. "Kyle, do you hear that? The ambulance is almost here. You and Cheryl are going to be fine."

It wasn't long afterward that Kyle and Cheryl were strapped to backboards, carried up the hillside and whisked away by ambulance to the nearest hospital. After giving their statements to the police officers working the accident, Bonnie and Paul, too, were finally free to leave.

Bonnie looked down at her wet, grubby clothes, then at Paul's which bore even more dirt and blood. "We'll mess up your car."

"Leather seats, they'll clean up. But you're shivering."

The rain was still light, but increasingly steady. The narrow straps of her top bared her shoulders and arms to the wet, rapidly cooling air. The wet cotton clung to her, and she was aware that the outline of her bra was visible through the fabric. She hadn't realized she was cold until he'd pointed it out. Now she noticed the goose bumps that prickled her arms.

Paul opened his trunk and drew out a thin plaid stadium blanket. He gave it a shake, then wrapped it around her shoulders. For just a moment, she allowed herself to lean against him, aware for the first time that her hands were shaking. He tightened his arms around her in a hug he seemed to need as badly as she did before settling her into the passenger seat. By the time he'd made it around the front of the car and into his own seat, the rain was coming down in earnest. Buckled into her seat, Bonnie drew the blanket more snugly around her as Paul started the car and drove carefully back onto the wet road.

"Do you think Cheryl will be okay?" she asked him, looking at the blood that streaked his clothes.

"She was banged up pretty good, but I think she'll be okay now that she's getting medical attention."

"I hope she'll recover quickly. I have to admit, I was pretty scared when they went off the road, and when I saw all the blood on her legs."

"Me, too."

She tilted her head, looking at his grim profile. "Really? You seemed so calm."

"All an outside act for Cheryl's sake. Inside, I was one blood spurt away from losing my cookies."

"You're a handy guy to have around in a crisis," she said lightly, trying to recapture the pleasant mood of earlier that day.

"So everyone keeps telling me," he said, staring

fiercely at the wet road ahead. "But sometimes I think it would be nice not to always be the go-to guy."

She bit her lip, frowning a little in response to his tone. Was he really tired of everyone depending on him, or was this just his reaction to the nerve-racking incident, much like her own shaking hands?

As if sensing her thoughts, he shook his head impatiently. "I don't mean that, of course. I'm glad we were there to help. Just shook me up, that's all."

"Me, too."

"Maybe we'd better skip the diner this trip," he said.

Putting irrelevant thoughts out of her mind—for now—she glanced down at her clothes. "I think that's best, since I look like a drowned rat."

He shot a very quick glance at her before focusing on the road again. "I wouldn't call you a drowned rat. A drowned kitten, maybe. Much cuter."

She smiled for the first time since they'd seen the motorcycle tumble off the road. "Oh, thanks so much."

His chuckle sounded very weary. Thinking of all that had happened that eventful day, she sat back in her seat and let him concentrate on the road ahead.

It was certainly late enough for dinner by the time Paul drove into the inn's parking lot. Bonnie directed him to drive around to the back, closer to her apartment entrance. Rain pounded the top of his car now and the surrounding mountaintops were illuminated by flashes of lightning followed moments later by a cranky grumble of thunder. Parking behind her little sedan, which was protected beneath a small carport, Paul reached behind his seat and retrieved a black umbrella.

"Hang on," he said, "I'll come around and get you. I only have the one umbrella."

She looked wryly down at her soiled clothing. "I don't think a little rain will hurt me."

As if to protest her use of the word *little,* a gust of wind threw a heavy wave of rain at the car, accompanied by another distant growl of thunder as the center of the storm blew nearer. "I'll come around," Paul repeated, then drew a deep breath and opened his door.

Leaving the damp blanket in the car, she clutched her small bag to her chest and huddled with him beneath the umbrella during the short dash to her door. None of the guests were out in this weather, of course, nor did she see any sign of her brother or sister. Kinley's car had been in the front lot, so she was probably in the parlor with the guests, keeping an eye on the weather reports.

Paul kept an arm around her bare shoulders to hold her close beneath the umbrella. He didn't release her even when they ducked beneath the small gable roof above her private entrance. He angled the umbrella to protect her from blowing rain as she fumbled with her key and unlocked the door.

Turning the doorknob, she looked up at him. "Come in with me. I'll make us something for dinner. Maybe the storm will let up some before you leave."

He motioned toward his grimy clothes. "I'm hardly fit company."

"Come in, Paul." She pushed open the door.

He hesitated only a heartbeat before dropping the umbrella on the porch, shuffling his wet feet on the outside mat and following her inside. She closed the door behind him.

Because her apartment formed a half basement beneath the south-facing inn, which had been built on a downward slope, she had windows only on two sides, west and north. To compensate for the lack of natural light, she'd chosen pale woods and bright colors for her decor. Her floor was made of large, diagonally placed porcelain tiles styled to resemble stone, so she didn't have to worry about tracking in a mess.

She kicked off her wet boots as soon as she was inside, tossed her purse on a chair and turned to study her guest. She couldn't help but shake her head at the sight of him. With his wet, tousled hair and his blood-and-dirt-streaked clothes, he was still incredibly appealing, but decidedly bedraggled.

"You'll be more comfortable if you take off your boots," she suggested. And then, remembering something, she said, "I'll be right back." She made a dash for the small laundry room attached to her kitchen.

She returned moments later carrying a pair of men's jeans and a large gray T-shirt. "Maybe you'd like to put on some clean, dry clothes before we eat. I can toss yours in the washer during dinner. I can't guarantee fit on these jeans, but they look close to your size, I think."

"You just happen to keep men's clothes on hand?"

"They're my brother's. His washer broke last week and he did a few loads of laundry here while he waited for a new part to be delivered. I found these in my dryer with a few other things yesterday and haven't had a chance to get them back to him yet. I'm sure he wouldn't mind if you borrow them for a couple of hours."

"Well, I—"

She grinned. "Strip, pal. I really can't look at those

bloody clothes of yours all during dinner. You can clean up in the spare bedroom. I'll change in my room."

She pointed him toward the correct door, then hurried into her own room to change. She made a quick call to Kinley to tell her she was home safely, and was assured that everything was fine upstairs. Kinley and Dan had decided to stay in one of the empty rooms overnight rather than brave the storm and drive back to her house.

"Everything's under control here," Kinley added. "We're playing charades in the parlor with some of the guests. Having a great time. You just take it easy the rest of the night. We'll call if we need you."

A few minutes later, Bonnie stood in her kitchen, having washed up and dressed quickly in a cotton top and skirt and slippers. Her hair was still a bit damp around the edges, but she'd left it down to dry. Paul wandered in a couple of minutes later, wearing his own socks and Logan's clothes, which fit him fairly well.

She reached for the dirty jeans and shirt he carried wadded in his hands. "I'll just throw these in the washer and then throw together something quick for dinner. Make yourself comfortable on the couch or at the table, if you prefer."

Rather than taking a seat, he was standing where she'd left him when she returned. "What can I do to help with dinner?"

Because he seemed genuinely to want to help, she set him to chopping tomatoes and a red onion while she sliced avocados, shredded white cheddar cheese and whisked together a vinaigrette for a Cobb salad.

"Maybe it's a good thing you're starting tomorrow night's class with knife skills," he said with a crooked smile as he washed the knife a few minutes later. "I'm a little slow when it comes to slicing and dicing."

"Better slow than sliced, yourself," she answered with a light shrug, retrieving romaine lettuce, cold chicken and boiled eggs from the fridge. "But maybe I can give you a few tips tomorrow night."

He reached out to brush her cheek with the back of his hand, making her almost drop the food on the floor. "I rather like this private lesson," he said in a low voice.

She cleared her throat and smiled up at him through her lashes. "You can have one of those anytime."

He chuckled and took a step back, as if moving away from temptation. "What can I do now?"

"I have some very good locally bottled white wine you can pour for us. I think we deserve a glass tonight, don't you?"

His reply was heartfelt. "Absolutely."

They took their time over the salads, sipping the wine slowly. They didn't talk a lot during the meal, and when they did they avoided discussing the traumatic motorcycle accident, chatting about his friend Tim's horse stables instead. After clearing away the dinner dishes, she transferred his clothes to the dryer. Paul carried his wineglass with him when he moved to sit on the deep-cushioned red couch in the open-floor-plan apartment.

The rain continued outside, with wind, rain and lightning putting on quite a show over the mountains. Paul checked the weather reports on his phone, relieved he'd found nothing more threatening than a thunderstorm warning. He'd called to check on Cassie, and said he was relieved to hear she was spending the turbulent night at her mom's.

"Did you tell her where you are?" Bonnie asked from the kitchen.

Looking over the back of the couch, he shook his head. "Not specifically. And she didn't ask."

She wondered if Cassie had her suspicions about where her dad was riding out the storm. Cassie had been a bit heavy-handed with her matchmaking Sunday, not so subtly leaving Bonnie and Paul alone together at his house. Awkward, but at least she didn't mind them spending time together.

She picked up the open bottle of wine on her way to join him. "More?" she asked, holding it over his glass.

Lightning flashed, thunder rumbled and he nodded with a faint smile. "Maybe half a glass. I'm not driving until my clothes are dry anyway."

She poured him a little more than half a glass, then added the same amount to her own. She found herself in no hurry for the dryer to buzz, and Paul looked content enough on her couch. She sat beside him, her full skirt arranged around her as she tucked her feet beneath her and half turned to face him.

"I'll bet Logan's down at his place worrying about any damage the storm could be doing. I'm sure there will be leaves and twigs thrown around, which he and Curtis, his assistant, will clean up in the morning, but I hope there's no real damage. It took us several weeks to fully recover from that ice storm last February."

"That was a bad one. Did you have much damage here?"

"Let's just say it took a bite out of our maintenance budget." She pictured her brother pacing the rooms of his cottage with Ninja at his side, peering out the windows to watch the storm, and she hoped he had enough sense to stay inside until the worst was past. He took nature's assaults on his landscaping quite personally at times.

"There's a heck of a lot that goes into running a business of this size, isn't there?"

Smiling wryly, she sipped her wine, then said, "There is. We didn't come into the operation completely unprepared, since all of us trained in various aspects of business. My degree, specifically, is in hotel management. Kinley majored in business, then real estate brokerage, and Logan is a computer whiz in addition to being talented with landscaping and maintenance. Dan calls him a true 'Renaissance man,' which always causes Logan to grumble because it makes him self-conscious."

"It sounds as though Bride Mountain Inn is in very competent hands."

"We certainly try." She pushed back her hair, feeling muscles that hadn't been used in a while remind her of the afternoon's activities. "It's been quite a day, hasn't it?"

Paul gave a little snort as he picked up his wineglass. "You can say that again. Not exactly the way I wanted our day of fun to turn out."

"Most of it was still fun," she assured him. "I loved our trail ride, I enjoyed meeting your friend and I've had a very pleasant dinner with you. All in all, that's not such a bad day."

Holding his wineglass loosely in his left hand, he reached out with his right to brush a strand of hair from her cheek. "You're the type to find the bright side in every situation, aren't you, Bonnie?"

"I want to," she confessed. "Nothing wrong with being an optimist, is there?"

Lightning glinted again through the windows, accompanied almost simultaneously by the boom of thunder, proving the storm had moved directly overhead now. The lights flickered, but stayed on, to her relief. The inn had an emergency generator system that kept the refrigerator and freezer running and operated a few lights upstairs, but it wasn't large enough to provide power for the entire inn. She reminded herself that Kinley and Dan were taking care of everything tonight, and that Logan was always on call if needed. This was her evening off, and it wasn't over yet.

Paul glanced toward the closest window, speaking up just a bit over the pounding of rain against the glass. "Nothing at all wrong with optimism. As long as it's tempered with a healthy dose of skepticism."

"I'm not naive, if that's what you mean. I just like to think everything works out the way it's supposed to eventually. It was certainly a good thing for Kyle and Cheryl that we were in the right place when the motorcycle went off the road."

"Or maybe if he hadn't been showing off for us, they wouldn't have gone off the road and been hurt at all," Paul countered. "So maybe we were in the wrong place at that time."

She laughed softly, shaking her head. "I think this is what they call a circular argument. I'd better get out of it before I wind up totally confused."

His lips quirked. "Cassie and I have gotten caught up in plenty of circular arguments during the years."

"And you liked it."

He shrugged, his lips twitching with a smile. "Maybe."

She took another sip of her wine, smiling at him over the rim of her glass.

Paul set his glass on the coffee table, then turned to her again. Almost absently, he reached out to toy with a lock of her hair that had curled tightly against her shoulder as it dried. "I appreciate your optimism," he said. "I'm always telling my students that if they can visualize success, they can likely achieve it. That's what you and your brother and sister have done here with the inn."

"We're getting there," she agreed, though her sudden awareness of his proximity, of the closeness of his hand to her breast made it more difficult to concentrate on their conversation. "We've, um, got a way to go before we completely break even from all the renovations we had to do before we opened, but that goal is in sight now. Another two or three years, maybe."

It was so hard to think coherently with him leaning closer to her, his jade eyes reflecting the flickering lightning from the window behind her. Her heart thudded against her chest so rapidly she thought he might have heard it if not for the thunder.

He took the wineglass from her suddenly nervous fingers and set it beside his own. "So you have at least a couple of more very busy years ahead. I'm glad you could take a few hours today to spend with me."

"So am I," she murmured as his mouth neared hers.

Finally their lips met, melded. His arms went around her and she wrapped hers around his neck, leaning eagerly into him. The tip of his tongue parted her lips, slipped just inside to taste her, slid slowly from side to side until she captured him, held him, deepened the kiss herself.

Oh, she had wanted this. Those previous kisses had been merely prelude to this one. Practice, maybe. This one…this one was serious.

His hands were buried in her hair now, fingers tangled in the curls. Electricity sizzled around them, her heartbeat pounded in her ears, mixing with the sounds of the rain and thunder so that she could almost wonder if the storm was inside or outside. The lightning dancing across her windows could just as believably been fireworks.

The lights flickered, once, twice. She moaned in protest when they blinked the third time and remained off. She didn't mind being in the dark with Paul, but she wondered if she needed to go upstairs and check on her guests.

As if in response to her thoughts, her phone chirped with a text.

Reluctantly, she drew back from Paul, who groaned softly when she broke off the kiss. The apartment was in deep shadows now with the storm darkening the skies outside, but she could see his rueful expression.

"I think you're being paged." He didn't sound annoyed, but sympathetically frustrated. Considering his longtime role as go-to family guy, he should certainly understand the need for her to check the message. She groped on the coffee table for her phone.

The text was from Kinley. Everything under control. Stay where you are.

"Do they want you to come up?"

She kept her phone in her hand, the glow of the screen providing light. "No. Kinley's in charge tonight.

She wanted to let me know I'm not needed at the moment."

"Maybe not upstairs," he said and reached for her again.

Dropping the phone on the table, she nestled against him, running a hand slowly up his chest. "The emergency generator doesn't provide power down here. I could light candles so we can see better."

"Or we could just depend on our sense of touch," he said, his voice warm with intimate humor.

Tongue tucked firmly in her cheek, she said gravely, "I suppose we really have no choice."

"No," he murmured, shifting his weight to press her back into the pillows. "No choice at all."

Her laugh was muffled by his kiss.

They put the sense of touch to very good use. Hands explored, caressed. Legs tangled, entwined. Bodies arched, shifted, strained. Every inch of her ached for his touch, and he seemed intent on satisfying that longing. He shifted onto his side on the couch and she lay facing him, one leg thrown over his, his hand sliding beneath her skirt to stroke her thigh. She had a hand beneath his borrowed T-shirt, her palm spread over his warm, taut skin, tickled by the light covering of hair across his chest. They kissed again, slowly, thoroughly, appreciatively.

She hadn't actually planned for the evening to go this far, but still she found herself in no hurry to bring it to an end. She wasn't thinking about the future now, about subtext or concerns, possibilities or potential disappointments. This night belonged solely to them—to her—and she wasn't ready for it to end.

Finally separating their lips by an inch or so, he cleared his husky throat. “Maybe I should go.”

Considering where his right hand was, and considering that she was pressed so snugly against him that she knew exactly how much he was enjoying this interlude, and considering that she had been participating very enthusiastically, she had to admit she was surprised by his words. Cassie was at her mother’s, so he would be returning to an empty house, possibly a dark house if the power outage extended that far. “Why?”

He grimaced expressively. “I think you know why.”

She appreciated that he wasn’t trying to rush her, despite his own obvious reluctance to stop. They would part on good terms if she sent him on his way now. Perhaps he would ask her out again soon, and maybe next time they could finish what they’d started tonight. Or maybe they could just finish it now, she thought, reaching up to cup his face in her hands and nibble his lips. She heard him inhale sharply, felt a little quiver run through him, and she had the satisfying suspicion that he was exerting a significant amount of willpower not to roll her beneath him.

“Bonnie,” he groaned against her mouth.

“You’re not really in a hurry to go, are you?” she asked, sliding her bare leg against his denim-covered one. “I mean, it’s still early. It wouldn’t even be dark out if it wasn’t storming.”

“I didn’t say I *want* to go,” he reminded her.

“Then don’t,” she said, making a sudden decision. She shifted into a sitting position, then stood and looked down at him. “Maybe you’d like to see the rest of my apartment?”

“I’ve wanted to see your bedroom for a while now.”

She laughed softly in response to his candid admission and took his hand as he rose. "Then by all means..."

"You're, um—?"

She broke in firmly. "I'm a big girl, Paul. And, as I said earlier, I'm not naive."

Clutching his shirt, she went up on tiptoe to face him. "I haven't had a vacation in almost three years. I haven't even had a day off in almost longer than I can remember. I am a single, unattached grown woman with a rare few hours for myself and a very handsome, occasionally charming man with whom to spend them. Now I could light a candle and we could play gin rummy, or we could adjourn to my bedroom with no strings and no regrets."

His smile flashed in the dim light. "Well, when you put it that way..."

They walked together toward her bedroom, with her leading the way. Just as they crossed the threshold, the power came on again, turning on the lights in the room behind them. Bonnie didn't bother to flip the bedroom switch, but closed the bedroom door instead. "Let's just pretend we didn't notice that, shall we?"

Tumbling with her to the bed, he said, "The only thing I see is you."

"Right answer," she assured him, and drew his mouth to hers.

Chapter Seven

The sizzling electricity in the room had nothing to do with the storm when Bonnie arched into Paul's eagerly roving hands. Hungry to taste the firm muscles she'd felt only through his clothes so far, she tugged at his shirt, pushed fabric out of the way, then pressed her parted lips to the warm skin she revealed.

Paul made a deep, rumbling sound when she circled one of his taut nipples with the tip of her tongue, and she laughed softly with pleasure against his chest. But then his hand slid beneath her skirt and her laughter changed to a breathless gasp.

His face buried in the curve of her throat, he nibbled, nipped and teased at her skin while sliding his fingers very slowly up her inner thigh. He kissed the upper curve of breast visible above the deep scoop of her top, which made her even more anxious to get all of their clothes out of the way. Her hands felt suddenly clumsy when she tugged off his shirt, wriggled out of her skirt, reached for the hem of her shirt and the button of his jeans, trying to do everything at once. Chuckling hoarsely, he helped her, tossing discarded garments haphazardly to the floor.

With the clothes out of the way, they slowed down, taking time to explore and savor. The steady rain against the window and the frequent rumble of thunder played a sultry soundtrack for their murmurs and moans, gasps and husky laughs. The lightning strobed through the room, revealing glittering eyes and glistening skin.

He pushed her to the edge of coherence with his skilled lips and fingers. He left no inch of her untouched, unappreciated. She took great satisfaction in knowing that she drove him to that same edge when she slid her palm down his flat abdomen and wrapped her hand around him. He inhaled sharply, then rolled to pin her beneath him, his mouth covering hers in a deep, thorough kiss.

Protection was dealt with swiftly, impatiently, and then he returned to her. She wrapped herself around him in welcome, her smaller form fitting quite nicely to his. And when finally he thrust into her, neither of them able to wait any longer, she was thrilled to note that their bodies meshed perfectly together. It was the last clear thought she had before waves of sheer sensation swept her to the peak of arousal and then threw her into the mindless turmoil of climax.

The storm outside had passed and the darkness in the room was due to the hour rather than the clouds by the time she trusted herself to speak with a semblance of lucidity. She didn't look at the clock, but she knew it was getting late, not that she cared.

She could tell by the way he sprawled loose-limbed beside her that Paul was as completely and contentedly sated as she. Nestling her cheek against his damp shoulder, she brushed a light kiss on his skin. "Are you awake?"

"I'm not entirely sure," he said, a smile in his voice. "I can't feel my feet yet."

She laughed softly. "I know what you mean. I think my knees have turned to jelly."

He pressed a kiss on top of her head. "Can you see the clock?"

"Probably, but I'm not in the mood to look at the moment. Are you in a hurry to leave?"

He tightened his arm around her. "Hell, no."

She raised her head to look at him. With the power back on, the security light outside the small, high bedroom window on the west wall cast a pale glow through the room, so that his face was shadowed, but clearly visible. His teeth gleamed with his smile and his eyes glittered as they met hers. "Hi."

She giggled. "Hi."

"Have I mentioned what a great time I've had today?"

"Me, too. You know, considering—"

He nodded to acknowledge her allusion to the motorcycle accident, but again didn't linger on the subject. "Think your sister knows I'm still down here?"

Bonnie wrinkled her nose in resignation. "Oh, I'm sure she does."

And her sister would rib her tomorrow, she added silently, prepared for the good-natured grilling. She supposed it was only fair, since she'd teased Kinley a bit during her whirlwind romance with Dan. Not that she was calling this a romance just yet, she reminded herself quickly. She had promised Paul there would be no strings, no regrets. That assurance had been meant for both of them. She was still very much taking a wait and see attitude about this developing connection. Waiting to see just what he had in mind after this magical night ended. Waiting to see if she was prepared to trust him to stick around if she let herself depend on him to be there.

"Do you mind about that?"

She brought her mind back to the topic. "Do I mind that my sister knows I have a life outside the inn and the family—or at least I try to, occasionally? No."

"Does she spend the night at the inn often?"

"Not very. When Dan's out of town, she stays fairly often to eat an early dinner with Logan and me and then heads home afterward. If we have an early event the next day, she'll sometimes stay over in the bedroom you changed in earlier. If anyone upstairs needs me at any time during the night, every guest has my number or there's an emergency alarm."

"So you're on call 24/7."

"Pretty much. That's why I don't feel at all guilty about having Kinley and Dan keeping an eye on everything upstairs tonight. We've got a crazy busy schedule for the next couple of months, through the end of September at least, and time off is going to be scarce until then for all of us."

She was letting him know, subtly, that this long, lazy afternoon had been a bit of an aberration. Not that he'd said anything about repeating it, but she figured she should warn him anyway. She could definitely make time for a dinner out, maybe a movie, maybe a few more nice evenings here, she thought with a ripple of secret anticipation, but entire afternoons could be tough to clear for the next couple of months.

He seemed to get the message. "So are you ever going to take a real vacation? More than a few free hours when you can grab them?"

"I've been thinking about it. Kinley and I have discussed maybe closing for a week or so during off-season after Christmas—late January, perhaps—and taking vacations. She'd go somewhere with Dan, of course."

"And you?"

"A couple of my friends from college have talked about getting together and taking a girls' cruise. I have to admit that's tempting."

"I see."

She couldn't quite interpret his tone, and his expression was hard to read. Maybe because of the dim light. "What about you?" she asked lightly. "Are you planning a vacation before school starts again?"

"Not this summer. Cassie and I have made a tradition of going to a beach for a week or ten days during summer vacations, but what with the wedding and all, there really hasn't been a chance this year. I won't have time to get away after the wedding, so I'm just enjoying a 'staycation' this summer. I've had a few teaching-related obligations, but for the most part I've had time to recharge and hang out with friends, which always makes it easier to face a new school year in the fall."

"When does your school start again?"

"I have to report back the last week of August. The students return the following week."

"We haven't talked much about your job," she realized aloud, propping her chin on his chest. "Do you like teaching?"

"Most of the time, yes. I teach calculus and advanced algebra, so I have mostly juniors and seniors who are on the college-bound path. A few of them even want to be there most days," he added with a wry chuckle.

"I bet you're their favorite teacher."

He laughed. "They like me well enough, but that honor generally goes to Ms. Lancaster, the speech and drama teacher. Let's just say she's attractive. And a genuinely nice person to boot. A natural-born teacher."

Despite his modesty, she suspected that Paul, with his warmth and humor and infectious smile, was high on the list of student favorites. She pushed her tousled hair out of her face before asking, "Did you always want to teach?"

He shrugged beneath her and reached out almost absently to twist a lock of her hair around his forefinger. He seemed to like doing that. "I always had an affinity for math. And teaching was a career that ensured me free time to spend with my daughter. It's worked out well for us."

Even though every inch of her body felt warm and soft from their lovemaking, she still thrilled a little when his hand brushed her breast as he played with her hair. She forced herself to focus on the conversation. "Do you have any plans beyond teaching high school? Moving into administration, maybe, or teaching at a college level?"

He gave a short laugh. "I've actually considered moving to China to teach. Or maybe North Dakota. Plan C is to be a beach bum in the Florida Keys."

Perhaps he'd thought she would laugh, too, at that latter improbable scenario. She tried, but wasn't quite successful. "You're moving away?"

The extent of her dismay at the possibility told her she hadn't been quite as successful as she'd thought in keeping her feelings for him under control. Had she really begun to hope that he would stick around, that maybe he wasn't looking forward to the freedom of his empty nest as much as he'd implied?

His shrug this time was more of an uncomfortable squirm. "Not anytime soon. I have a contract to teach for another year here. I've just been thinking about all the options ahead for me now that I won't be responsible for anyone but myself for the first time since—well, since longer than I can remember."

She wasn't oblivious to the fact that settling down and having more children had not been one of the options he'd listed. He really did see her as just a summer fling, she thought with a hard swallow. It was a good thing she knew that for certain now, just in case she'd secretly started hoping for more.

She had options of her own, she reminded herself, though perhaps hers were a bit more limited considering the hours she spent working. But that was her choice, and she didn't regret it, even though most of the men she met were either grooms-to-be or honeymooners. With an occasional sexy, contentedly single father-of-the-bride thrown in, she thought with a light sigh.

She rolled and reached for the robe she usually kept at the foot of the bed, finding it on the floor instead. It would take her a few minutes to put the tangled bedclothes back in order, she thought with a somewhat sheepish smile.

"Where are you going?"

Balancing on still slightly unsteady legs, she wrapped the robe around herself and loosely tied the sash. "The bathroom, and then to the kitchen for water. I'm thirsty."

He pushed a hand through his hair, and she could see resigned acceptance on his face that the evening was drawing to an end. "I guess I'd better head home soon. I know you'll have an early start tomorrow."

She didn't try to detain him this time. "I'll bring your clothes. Maybe they dried enough before the power went out for you to wear them home."

"I'm sure they'll be fine."

Suddenly needing to be busy, she turned on one heel and moved a little too quickly away from the rumpled bed.

Paul left not long afterward. His clothes were still damp, but he assured her they were fine for the short drive home. His boots squished a bit when he shoved his feet in them, but he merely shrugged and said he'd set them out to dry when he got home. It was still raining, but very lightly now.

Still wearing her robe, she stood by the door to see him off. "Be careful driving down the mountain on these wet roads," she said automatically. Compared to the steep grades they'd been on earlier, Bride Mountain was little more than a tall hill, but still the road could be slick when wet.

"Yes, I will." One hand on the doorknob, he paused. "About the farmers' market tomorrow morning..."

"I'll be at the main entrance at just before eight, waiting for any class members who can be there. So far, I've heard from two who said they could make it, Nora and Jennifer."

She saw what might have been the faintest wince from him when she said the latter name, though she couldn't be sure. "I'm afraid I can't join you. I have a meeting at school district HQ in the morning. But I'll be in class tomorrow evening."

Her first reaction was disappointment that she wouldn't see him there, but then she decided maybe it was best. That would give her a few hours to prepare herself to greet him in front of the others. "I'll see you at six, then."

"I'll be on time," he promised, and leaned over to kiss her lingeringly.

She cleared her husky throat when he finally drew back. "Good night, Paul."

He winked at her and let himself out. Only after she'd locked up behind him did Bonnie realize that neither of them had said anything about getting together again outside the class.

Paul told himself he understood completely why Bonnie wouldn't want to give any hint to the class that anything had happened between the two of them since last week. She was professional to the core when she stood in front of her group Tuesday evening. Her teaching manner was warm, casual, encouraging, and she treated each participant the same, whether they were experienced in the kitchen or total novices. Or had been in her bed only hours before, he thought, receiving another sweetly impersonal smile that included him in with all the other class members.

"Now that we've practiced safe knife skills and had a little break, let's get to cooking," she said as they stood shoulder to shoulder at the long prep bar in the center of the kitchen, three to a side, Bonnie at one end. "Everyone put on your apron and pick up your Santoku knife."

"Paul looks awfully cute in his apron," Nora said with a giggle. "Maybe he could help you demonstrate again and the rest of us could just watch and admire."

"As cute as he is, I want you all to leave the class with a few new skills," Bonnie said easily, barely glancing at Paul as she spoke. "Everyone ready to carefully chop and dice?"

Yeah, Bonnie was doing a great job of hiding any personal feelings she might have for him, Paul thought, roughly tying his apron strings behind his back. Someone who didn't know better might think they hardly knew each other at all. Just a teacher and a student who was no more special to her than any of the others in the small class. Wasn't it just great how damned good she was at pretending she didn't give two flips about him?

Suddenly aware that he was scowling, he smoothed his expression immediately, hoping if anyone had noticed they would attribute it to him trying to memorize the cooking instructions. She talked enthusiastically about bok choy and shiitake mushrooms, about cherry tomatoes and zucchini and radishes and cucumbers and whatever else she'd procured from the market that morning, and he tried very hard to pay attention. But how was he supposed to care about fruits and vegetables when Bonnie stood there looking so fresh and pretty in her colorful skirt and red apron, her golden hair pinned tidily back from her face? When she waved a hand in the air to emphasize a point and all he could think about was how softly those fingers had caressed him last night? When she lifted a spoon to her lips to taste a broth, and he could only remember the sweet, spicy taste of *her?*

Maybe this class hadn't been such a clever idea on his part, after all.

"Don't you agree, Paul?"

The sound of his name made him blink. "Um, what?"

Jennifer leaned close to him, speaking quietly into his ear while Bonnie continued with the demonstration. "I said, doesn't this food look delicious? Bonnie is really a talented chef. I'm not sure why she's content to spend her whole life here in western Virginia when she could be making a name for herself in New York or Boston or even California."

"Bonnie loves it here. The inn has been in her family for several generations. She told my daughter that she has wanted to run this inn ever since she was a little girl visiting here with her mother and brother and sister."

"Hmm. Well, I was born and grew up within fifteen miles of here, got married right out of high school and divorced last year. I'm about ready to see something besides backwoods and mountains."

"Shh," Nora murmured chidingly to Jennifer. "I'm trying to hear how long to broil the bok choy."

"It will all be in the handouts," Jennifer said with a shrug, though she turned again to pay attention to the instructions.

Paul certainly hoped so. Not because Jennifer had distracted him from the lesson, but because his own convoluted emotions had.

The class ended with everyone filling small plates of the dishes they had prepared. While they sampled, Bonnie answered questions and chatted easily.

"In our final class next week, we'll talk about produce you can buy in winter, and how to preserve summer goodies to enjoy all year," she promised them. "And I'll be at the market that morning at eight."

"These grilled peaches could be the best thing I've ever put in my mouth," Lydia enthused, her eyelids half-closed in ecstasy. "I've got to try making them."

"Thank you," Bonnie said. "I love them, myself."

"Bonnie, we must put these on the menu for the anniversary party for my parents," Nora insisted. She glanced at Paul as she explained, "My parents are celebrating their fortieth anniversary next month and my sister and I are hosting an intimate reception for them here at the inn on a Sunday afternoon. Only thirty of their closest friends. I've asked Bonnie to handle the catering, which she's graciously agreed to do."

Paul remembered that Bonnie had said she would be very busy for the next couple of months with bookings that apparently included Nora's party, not to mention his daughter's wedding events. He guessed he'd never realized quite how much work went on behind the scenes of a busy bed-and-breakfast that also catered to outside events, and even provided occasional cooking classes. He thought of Nora's joking comment last week that the Carmichael siblings were married to the inn. Seemed true enough, considering Kinley was the only one involved in a serious relationship, and that with a man who traveled quite a bit.

It was rather ironic that just as he found himself with lots of options and quite a bit of free time ahead after his daughter's wedding and the Bauer family's move, he had become involved with a woman with almost overwhelming commitments to this particular place. True, they were both trying to keep their connection informal—as she had said, "no strings, no regrets," exactly the way he wanted things between them—but even as he stood in her kitchen with her and the five other members of the class, all he could think about was when he could next manage to be alone with her.

"So, do you want to walk with us out to our cars or are you staying to help the teacher 'clean up'?" Jennifer asked Paul as the other women began to gather their things and drift out.

Paul suppressed a wince at the knowing tone in Jennifer's slightly catty question. Maybe he hadn't been quite as skilled as Bonnie at masking his personal interest in her. But, whatever. It wasn't as if he were trying to hide his relationship with her. "I'll hang around if she needs some help," he said easily.

Joining them in time to overhear, Bonnie smiled. "Actually, you can stash some things in the high cabinets for me again. A tall man is even handier than a step stool," she added with a laugh to Jennifer.

Jennifer sighed gustily. "Don't I know it. Okay, see y'all next week. Thanks for another fun class, Bonnie."

"I think she suspects something is going on between us," Paul said when he and Bonnie were alone. "I didn't say anything..."

Bonnie shrugged as she busily cleared and wiped

counters. "It's not as if we're sneaking around to see each other on the sly," she said, unconsciously parroting his thoughts. "And it's not as if I'm grading the class, so it doesn't really matter if I have a teacher's pet," she added with a wink over her shoulder that warmed his blood.

He couldn't resist catching her around the waist and lifting her into his arms for a kiss. It had been almost twenty-four hours since he'd kissed her last and he was hungry for another taste of her. She cooperated eagerly.

"Hey, Bon, can you— Oh, uh, sorry."

Breaking apart, Paul and Bonnie both turned to the back door which Logan had just thrown open. Logan looked both embarrassed and a little displeased to have caught them in a kiss, or at least that was the way Paul interpreted the other man's stern expression. He didn't really know Bonnie's brother, having only seen him around the inn a couple of times, but he suspected it was never easy to tell what Logan was really thinking.

Beside him, Bonnie tucked her hair behind her right ear, and while her cheeks were suspiciously pink, her voice was normal enough when she asked, "What do you need, Logan?"

He seemed reluctant to answer for a moment, and Paul half expected him to make an excuse and leave. Instead, Logan sighed and came farther into the kitchen. "I've got a damned rose thorn in my back and I can't reach it. Mind taking it out for me?"

He turned and raised the hem of his T-shirt to show her his back. Paul winced in sympathy. The thorn had broken off just beneath the angrily inflamed skin almost directly between Logan's shoulder blades. A few drops of blood had scabbed around the thorn, which must have gone right through his thin cotton shirt and broken off when he'd pulled away from the rosebush. Had to hurt.

Expecting Bonnie to sympathize with her brother, Paul was a bit startled when she seemed to be struggling with a laugh. "Logan! How on earth did you manage to do this?"

He muttered a rather sheepish explanation. "Ninja stole a hammer from my toolbox and hid it under that big rosebush at the side of my house. I had to crawl under to get it, and the damned bush attacked me."

"Sit down where I can reach you. I'll get the first aid kit."

"I don't need first aid, just take out the damned thorn."

Bonnie seemed not at all cowed by her older brother's snarl. "You can growl all you want, but I'm going to put an antibiotic ointment on it so it doesn't get infected. Now pull off your shirt and sit down."

Logan tugged the shirt over his head to reveal a tanned torso ridged with muscles Paul tried not to envy. He was in reasonably good shape but dang…

Logan settled on a stool at the prep bar. "You got any sisters, um—?"

"Paul. And no, I was an only."

"They're a pain in the butt."

"Oh, be quiet," Bonnie said, emerging from a large pantry with a first aid kit in her hands. "You know you love us. Besides, who would pull this thorn from your back if it weren't for me? Ninja?"

"What kind of dog is Ninja?" Paul asked, leaning against the counter to watch as Bonnie ministered to her brother.

"Mutt," Logan answered succinctly. "He showed up as a stray and decided to hang around."

Bonnie giggled. "Kinley says he's part rottweiler, part Lab, part imp and part demon. He's really a very sweet dog, but he has a mischievous sense of humor that gets him in trouble."

Paul quirked an eyebrow at her. "A sense of humor?"

"Oh, definitely. He loves to steal things and hide them, like Logan's hammer. He gets a special kick out of teasing Kinley, because he knows it makes her crazy."

"Uh-huh."

He must have sounded skeptical, because Bonnie shot him a smile. "You'd have to meet him to understand. I swear there are times I think he's almost human."

"He's a dog, Bonnie."

She leaned close to her brother, using a pair of tweezers she'd swished in alcohol to dig for the broken thorn. "He's a very smart dog. And you love him."

"Ouch! Damn it, are you pulling the thorn out or pushing it deeper in?"

"It's out." She showed him the grisly evidence then treated the minor wound with ointment and an adhesive bandage to keep it clean. She then gave him a smacking kiss on the top of his head, proving again that she was not at all intimidated by Logan's impatient posturing.

Logan grumbled again, but Paul saw him hiding a grin as he donned his shirt. "Thanks, Bon."

"You're welcome. Keep it clean."

"Up to date on your tetanus shots?" Paul asked. "I knew a guy who got tetanus from stepping on a barberry thorn. Nasty."

Logan shared a look with his sister before answering. "I'm current on all my shots."

Bonnie changed the subject. "Logan, Paul's daughter is getting married here in a few weeks. Paul, Logan and his crew will handle all the outdoor preparations for the wedding."

"We've been told you do beautiful set-ups," Paul said, thinking of Cassie's raves about the photographs she'd been shown.

Rising from the stool, Logan glanced from Paul to his sister and back again with his dark brows drawn down over narrowed hazel eyes. Still, he spoke cordially enough. "We aim to please."

Without further elaboration, Logan turned to his sister. "Tomorrow morning Curtis and I will be taking down that fir branch that was broken in the storm last night. I'm going to rope off the area around it, but be sure and tell the guests not to come back beyond the gazebo until we give the all clear."

"I will. Y'all be careful."

"Just have to keep Ninja from hiding my pole saw." Logan gave an upward chin nod to Paul as he headed for the door. "Later."

Paul frowned when the door closed behind Logan. He glanced at Bonnie. "Looked as though he hurt his leg, too. Did you notice he was limping a little?"

Bonnie busied herself putting away the first aid supplies. "That's an old limp from surgery on his leg when he was younger. It's a little more noticeable when he's tired."

"I don't think he likes me."

"He only just met you," she pointed out as she squirted disinfectant on the prep island and wiped it with a towel. "Logan takes his time to decide if he likes or dislikes someone."

Paul remembered her brother's frown when he'd walked in to find them kissing, of the undertones in the other man's voice when he'd commented about Paul being the father of a bride. "He probably thinks I'm too old for you."

"That's ridiculous. I don't choose my friends based on age. And you're not that much older than I am, anyway. It's not as if you're old enough to be my father."

True. But still she was a bit closer to his daughter's age than to his, Paul thought glumly. He didn't know why it bugged him for Bonnie to refer to him so blithely as her "friend." They *were* friends, right? He was quite sure they would remain friendly even after their physical relationship changed, as it inevitably would. Wasn't that his pattern?

He was becoming grumpy again, he thought, pushing a hand through his hair. He hadn't gotten a lot of sleep last night. "So what's your schedule now? Are you finished for the day?"

She glanced at the clock and he followed her gaze, noting that it was almost nine. "I should check on my guests and then I have a few things to get ready for breakfast in the morning before I can turn in tonight."

And he was detaining her, he thought, though she would never say so. "I'll get out of your way. I'll call you tomorrow, okay?"

She smiled. "Absolutely okay."

Wrapping his hand at the back of her head, he pulled her toward him and kissed her with a thoroughness meant to leave her thinking about him long after he left. He knew it would certainly torment him.

* * *

Darn that alarm!

The nagging buzzer roused her at the usual 5:30 a.m. from a dream filled with teeth-rattling kisses and moan-coaxing caresses. Thoughts of Paul filled her head as she climbed from the bed and showered and dressed, then hovered at the back of her mind while she prepared and served breakfast, checked out departing guests, welcomed new ones, checked on rooms and ordered supplies. A screen print of a horse on a guest's T-shirt elicited a vision of Paul sitting tall in the saddle. A glimpse of a vacationing couple kissing in the garden made her knees go weak with memories. Folding sheets from the clothes dryer made her think of how hot he'd looked sprawled across her own.

She wasn't sure she'd had a crush this strong since her sophomore year of college when she'd had a thing for a grad student who'd been working as a teaching assistant in one of her science labs. Every time he'd smiled at her, she'd blushed and trembled, and he'd been well aware of it. He'd romanced her for a heady three weeks, then moved on to the next impressionable teenager. She'd been somewhat disillusioned, but not heartbroken, as she'd figured out rather quickly that he was a player. It wasn't long after that when Kinley's selfish jerk of a husband had walked out, after which both Kinley and Bonnie had decided to focus on making futures for themselves as independent, self-sufficient women—just as their mother had done after their father walked out on her. Not that either Bonnie or Kinley had sworn off men; they'd simply decided separately to make sure they could take care of themselves before they tied their futures to anyone else.

So, here she was, exactly where she wanted to be. Standing in the inn's laundry room folding sheets and daydreaming about rolling on them with the father of one of the inn's clients. She bit back a sudden bark of wry laughter.

"Something funny?" Rhoda asked, entering with a basket of soiled towels. "Is the dryer telling jokes now?"

"Something like that." Bonnie set the neatly folded sheet on a shelf. "You can throw those in the washer. It's empty."

Rhoda reached for the additive-free detergent they used on the inn linens. "The dishwasher is making that funny sound again. You might get Logan to look at it when he gets a minute."

Bonnie sighed. If it wasn't one thing, it was another. They'd just had to buy a new vacuum, and a new restaurant-quality dishwasher was definitely not in the budget this month. If it became necessary, something else would have to be cut.

"I'll tell him. Maybe he or Curtis can find the source of the noise and fix it without calling a repairman."

Rhoda nodded. "It's still working for now, so I guess there's no real rush."

Bonnie picked up the mini-tablet she'd gotten into the habit of carrying during the day to make notes, checklists, shopping lists and anything else that kept her organized. She added the dishwasher to her to-do list. "Anything else?"

"Not at the moment."

"I'm going to take a lunch break, then." It was nearly two, and she was hungry. "Have you eaten?"

"Not hungry. I'll get something later."

Nodding, Bonnie moved toward the doorway.

"You got plans to see that nice-looking man again anytime soon?" Rhoda asked, detaining her a moment longer. "You notice we managed to handle things around here for an entire half day without you, and the world didn't end. Wouldn't hurt you to plan another afternoon off before long."

Rhoda was always fussing about how many hours Bonnie spent working. Though Kinley and Logan worked very hard, and put in plenty of long hours, themselves, Bonnie was aware that she logged the most time in the inn. Unless something came up that required his attention, Logan usually closed himself into his cottage after work, or drove into town for a beer with friends. Kinley divided her energies between the inn and her part-time real estate job, and was now building a life with Dan away from work. Bonnie was the one who tended to work almost from the time she woke until she crawled back into bed at night.

Could she find a way to make a life for herself outside the inn, like her sister was doing? Yesterday had been a good start, she assured herself. And yet—

"You know how busy our schedule is for the rest of the summer, Rhoda," she said mildly. "I'll take a few hours off when I can, so don't nag, okay?"

"Fine. Work yourself to the bone, see where that gets you," Rhoda grumbled, punching the start button on the washer with more force than necessary.

Bonnie didn't linger to argue. "Call if you need me."

"Don't we always?"

Chapter Eight

As she often did, Bonnie cooked an early dinner that evening for Logan and Kinley. Dan joined them when he could, but he had left that morning on another overnight assignment. Because she'd eaten a late lunch, Bonnie wasn't particularly hungry, but Logan and Kinley made short work of the baked chicken and roasted vegetables she served. They talked about work during the meal, primarily discussing several large upcoming events and conferring about some pending decisions. Logan had been talking to a contractor friend about the restrooms and dressing rooms they envisioned beneath the back deck, and his friend had suggested some good ideas.

"Winter is his downtime, construction-wise, and he said he'd work up some estimates for us to keep at least part of his crew busy. He looked at that sketch of what we wanted and he said it looked feasible to him."

"We could put off the koi pond until next year," Kinley said, pushing her empty plate away. "If Dan's article in *Modern South* accomplishes what we hope, we'll have quite a few new bookings for next summer, so additional restroom facilities are probably needed more than pretty fish. Don't you agree, Bon?"

"What?" She'd been listening to the conversation, Bonnie assured herself. But maybe her attention had wandered just a little.

Kinley frowned. "The dressing rooms," she prodded. "We should talk to Logan's friend."

"Oh, yes. Absolutely."

"So what's on your mind tonight, hmm? Or should I ask, *who's* on your mind?"

"Don't tease me tonight, Kinley, I'm too tired." She smiled wryly as she spoke in a joking tone, but she was mostly serious. It had been a long day and tomorrow would be another one, followed by a wedding rehearsal tomorrow evening, another on Friday, a wedding Saturday morning and another ceremony Saturday evening.

They rarely scheduled two weddings in one day, but because both were relatively small, low-key events, they'd been able to work it out this time when the morning bride had begged them to accommodate her on fairly short notice. The military groom was being deployed overseas in a couple of weeks, and they had decided to tie the knot before he left rather than after his return, as had been the original plan.

Logan had fussed, of course, at all the set-ups and take-downs he and Curtis and part-time helper Zach would have to do this weekend, but he'd get it done and the clients would hardly be aware of how much work went on behind the scenes of their celebrations.

"He's too old for you."

Logan's grumble broke into Bonnie's rambling thoughts. "Who?"

"That Paul guy," her brother replied, obviously confirming Paul's suspicion about Logan's misgivings.

Bonnie shook her head. "He's not too old for me. He was very young when his daughter was born, so he's not the typical father of the bride."

"So? He could end up a grandfather in a year or two. You really want to get involved with a grandfather before you even turn thirty?"

She had to admit the question took her aback for a moment, but she shook it off quickly. If Cassie did have a baby within the next two years, Paul would be a young, fit, sexy grandfather. But that was far from her concerns at the moment.

"We made an agreement when we all went into business together, remember?" she asked, addressing the firm question to both her siblings. "Since we spend so much time together and live in such close proximity, it's especially important that we maintain our boundaries, both professionally and personally. This is me, protecting my boundaries. Back off, both of you."

Kinley and Logan exchanged looks that expressed both surprise that their usually easygoing younger sister had snapped at them, and maybe concern that she'd felt defensive enough to do so. She didn't want to get into it any more just then. "I'm going up to make sure everything is set up in the parlor for the guests. There's lemon pie in the fridge. Help yourself if you want and let yourself out when you're done."

She didn't have to feel remorseful about leaving them there, she assured herself as she stalked out the door and up the steps to the back door of the inn. It wasn't as if her sister and brother were company. Still, she felt a bit guilty as she pasted on a hostess smile and headed for the parlor. She was usually the peacemaker in the family. But that didn't mean her older siblings had open permission to tell her what to do—or whom to do it with, she added indignantly. Even if she had her own questions about whether she and Paul had a future together, that decision was strictly between the two of them.

She was just about to turn in that night when Paul called. Seeing his name on her phone screen made her smile even as her pulse rate jumped. She sat back on the bed, curled her feet beneath her and lifted the phone to her ear. "Hello?"

"Hi. I hope it's not too late to call."

"I'm still awake," she assured him. "I was just getting ready for bed."

A moment of silence followed her comment and she wondered a bit self-consciously if he was picturing her in bed. She was suddenly thinking of him that way, which made her shift restlessly against the headboard and resist an impulse to fan her cheeks with her free hand.

"I didn't know when to call so I wouldn't interrupt your work, but I figured you'd be done by now." His voice sounded just a bit deeper than usual. "How was your day?"

"Busy. Yours?"

"I took the twins and a few of their friends to the lake for a cookout and swim."

"That had to be interesting in your Mustang," she teased.

He chuckled. "I rented a seven-passenger van for the day. They filled the seats."

"Sounds like fun."

"It was…interesting. They flirted and giggled and roughhoused, and then at the end of the day the girls cried all the way back while the guys postured and mocked them."

"Why did the girls cry?"

"Because the twins are moving away and Jenna and her friends want to extract as much angst and drama as possible from the next month."

Bonnie smiled, remembering how her own friends had relished dramatic performances at that age. "It was very noble of you to serve as their chaperone today."

She could almost hear him shrug. "I want to spend a little time with them during these last weeks, too," he admitted. "Though I managed not to burst into noisy tears when I dropped them off at their house."

She laughed. "Very stoic of you."

"We manly men are tough like that."

"Of course. Cassie didn't go with you guys today?"

"No, she had classes. She said if I talked to you I should tell you she's going to call tomorrow to set up a time when you can get together for a fitting. Apparently she's got your dress to a point where she needs you to try it on."

"I can't wait to see it. I could probably clear a couple of hours Sunday afternoon. If she needs to see me before then, she'll have to stop by here for a quick consultation."

"Really busy, huh?"

She explained about the two weddings scheduled for Saturday, and he offered both congratulations and sympathy, making her smile again. "By the way," she said, "Cassie's friend Danielle and her fiancé met with Kinley this afternoon and booked the inn for the third weekend in May. They've already hired a wedding planner, who came with them. I met with them only briefly, but I'm sure it's going to work out great."

Danielle wasn't using the same planner as Cassie, a nice man Bonnie and Kinley had collaborated with several times before, but rather someone new to the area. Alexis Mosley, who had appeared to be close to Bonnie's age, had purchased her business from a wedding planner who'd recently retired. She had seemed quite nice and highly competent. Kinley, needless to say, had made it very clear that they would always welcome Alexis and her future clients at Bride Mountain Inn.

"I'm glad Cassie was able to recommend you to her friend. Maybe Danielle will also bring in word-of-mouth business."

"We'll take all the business we can get," she replied cheerfully. "It would be nice if we could spread it out a bit, rather than mostly in a span of a few weeks, but we're not too choosy."

"I was going to ask if you have time for dinner or a movie sometime in the next few days, but it sounds as though that's a long shot this week. Maybe we can get together sometime next week," he said, sounding resigned.

"I'm free Monday evening for dinner."

"Pencil me in."

She chuckled at the dated phrase. "I'll type you in," she corrected. "And then I'll hit Save."

"Yeah, do that."

"And maybe I'll see you on Sunday, if that's when Cassie wants to get together."

"That would be nice. I'll let you get some rest now. Just wanted to say hi."

"Hi," she said, smiling softly in response to the intimate memory that crept into her mind with the word.

"Sleep well, Bonnie."

He disconnected before she could respond. Could he possibly suspect that she expected to lie awake for a while yet, thinking about him, wondering what would happen between them, and breathlessly anticipating the next time she could see him?

"Cassie, this is going to be the most beautiful dress I've ever owned." Late Sunday afternoon, Bonnie twisted in front of the full-length mirror in the bedroom of Paul's home that Cassie had commandeered as a sewing room. She peered over her shoulder at the low-cut back of the leaf-green, cap sleeve sheath, blinking a bit at the way the fabric hugged the curve of her hips and bottom.

This was a new dress shape for her, formfitting, revealing a triangular swath of back and a tasteful amount of cleavage. The waist nipped in to give her an almost classic hourglass shape, and the hem was just short enough to make her legs look surprisingly long beneath the sleek silhouette. A pair of heels would make it look even better, she thought, rising slightly on tiptoes and admiring the result.

Cassie dimpled in pleasure, smiling around the pin she held in her mouth. She removed it to slide it carefully into the fabric at Bonnie's right side, making a minute adjustment to the fit. "That's better. Definitely wear heels. They don't have to be stilettos, but at least a nice two-inch."

"Would you wear a necklace with it?"

Cassie shook her head, making her loose strawberry blond ponytail wobble precariously. "A bracelet and earrings. No necklace."

"You're the designer," Bonnie conceded, amused. "That's part of presenting your garments, isn't it? Styling the model?"

"Yes." Cassie looked as though she couldn't wait to get started with that. "So, I'll advise you to leave your hair down in loose waves and wear a bright blusher that brings out your eye color. Those blue eyes are gorgeous."

Now it was Bonnie's turn to dimple. "Thank you."

"Just calling it like I see it. There's nothing more I need to do today, so you can put your other clothes on. Be careful of the pins. Just lay the dress over that chair. I'll go pour us some tea while you dress."

"Sounds good." Not to mention that she knew Paul was waiting downstairs for them. She'd barely had time to greet him when she'd arrived and had been rushed upstairs by his daughter for the fitting. And now that that was out of the way…

She glanced at her watch, sighing at how little free time she had before she had to rush back to the inn. Carefully peeling off the mostly finished dress, she draped it over the designated chair and dressed quickly in the top and skirt she'd worn over. Pushing a hand through her hair to smooth it, she moved down to the kitchen, her heart already beating rather rapidly in anticipation.

She found Cassie pouring iced tea into three tall glasses at the table. Paul stood by the counter. He turned when Cassie walked in, grinning, a chip-and-dip tray cradled between his hands. He set it on the table with a flourish. "Just in case you want a snack," he said.

Lifting an eyebrow in response to his tone, she glanced from him to the tray. The center bowl held a creamy dip topped with chopped, roasted red peppers. Kale chips surrounded the bowl, appearing to be perfectly roasted.

"Kale chips tossed with olive oil, garlic, lemon juice, red pepper flakes and sea salt and baked until crispy," he said, speaking nonchalantly. "Served with roasted red pepper yogurt dip seasoned with a little smoked paprika."

"You made this?"

"All by himself," Cassie assured her with a proud laugh. "Can you believe it? Dad making kale chips? Roasting red peppers and making dip with them?"

"I'm impressed," Bonnie assured him.

He held a chair for her. "Maybe you should taste it first."

Moments later, she dabbed her mouth with the paper napkin Cassie had set out beside the snack plates. "Definitely impressed. This is delicious, Paul. I'm giving you extra credit for the class."

Cassie hooted.

Paul laughed. "You're not even grading the class."

"Okay, I'll give you metaphorical extra credit. This is really good."

Paul scooped dip onto a chip. "I found the recipe on one of those internet sites you recommended."

He popped the chip into his mouth, chewed and swallowed. "It is pretty good, if I say so myself."

Cassie munched appreciatively. "It's so nice that Dad's learning how to cook more healthily now that he's going to be living here entirely on his own. I'm glad he's taking your class, Bonnie."

She smiled across the table at him, receiving a wink in return. "So am I."

"Danielle called me and said she booked the inn for her wedding. She's so excited."

"I'm glad. And thank you for the referral."

"Of course. I've been telling all my friends how nice it is to work with you. I'll bet that article Kinley's boyfriend wrote for *Modern South* will help with business, too. I read it online this morning. The history of the place is really interesting. Is it really haunted?"

Bonnie suppressed a wince as she thought of her sister's probable reaction to that question. Not to mention Logan's. "No, it isn't haunted."

"The ghost bride, right?" Paul nodded knowingly. "I heard about her once. Don't remember where."

Bonnie gave them a quick summary of the old legend about a young woman who had overcome many obstacles to be with the love of her life, only to die tragically the night before her long-planned wedding. It had been said that she had haunted Bride Mountain whenever true love was present there, smiling a blessing at couples who had found the happiness together she'd known too briefly with her love. Some had embellished the story to add that when a couple saw the bride, it meant they would live happily ever after together.

Cassie sighed deeply. "It's such a sad story, isn't it?"

"Most old legends are," her father pointed out.

"But it's sweet. Have you ever seen her, Bonnie?"

Bonnie smiled and shook her head. "No. But of course, I haven't been in a serious relationship while I've lived in the inn."

Paul looked at her quizzically. "Surely you don't believe she really exists."

"And why not?" Cassie demanded. "There are more things on this earth than can be explained with mathematics, Daddy."

"Yes, but—"

Ignoring him, Cassie turned to Bonnie. "Have you ever known anyone who saw her?"

She hesitated only a moment, then answered candidly. "My great-uncle Leo and great-aunt Helen swore they both saw her the night Uncle Leo proposed. They didn't talk about it much, and almost never outside the family, but they were convinced she smiled at them in the flower garden."

"Oh my gosh, that's so romantic!"

"Logan thinks Uncle Leo made up the story to entertain me because I loved hearing it as a child. Kinley says maybe they saw a wisp of fog and got carried away by their joy that evening into believing it was the bride. I was the only one who believed him unconditionally."

"And you still do, don't you?" Cassie challenged her.

Bonnie merely smiled.

"Have you considered using the legend for advertising purposes?" Paul asked, picking up his tea glass. "I haven't seen it mentioned on your website."

"Kinley and Logan worry that having a ghost story formally attached to the inn would attract the wrong kind of crowd, those looking for haunted house thrills they would not receive, or deter potential guests simply looking for a peaceful getaway. As for myself, I'm just reluctant to use that sweet story my great-uncle used to tell me for advertising fodder. So we rely on our excellent service, our beautiful setting and our comfortable accommodations to sell ourselves to potential guests."

"And someday you and your brother and sister can tell your children about the sweet legend attached to the family inn," Cassie said. "Maybe someday one of you will even see her in person."

"Maybe we will." A bit of kale seemed to stick in Bonnie's throat. She took several swallows of her tea, then stood. "I really have to get back to the inn now. I can't count on the bride to serve sandwiches for me."

"I have to run too, to make a phone call," Cassie said. "Bye, Bonnie. I'll call later to set up a time to deliver your dress and take your picture in it, okay?"

"Yes, I'll look forward to it. And if I don't see you before, I'll see you next Sunday at your shower."

"I can't wait." With a final quick wave, Cassie dashed out of the room.

Paul's gaze met Bonnie's, and his expression turned suddenly wry. "I think that was her oh-so-subtle way of giving me a chance to kiss you good-night."

"I had the same suspicion," she agreed with a laugh. "And since she went to so much trouble…"

She stepped closer to him and lifted her face. He did not hesitate to take her up on the silent invitation.

Eventually the kiss had to end, of course. "We're still on for tomorrow night?" he asked as they reluctantly separated.

"Yes. Is seven-thirty okay? That will give me time to finish all my chores and get ready."

"Seven-thirty is good for me."

"Fine. I'll cook. You bring wine."

"Red or white?"

"Surprise me."

"I'll certainly try," he murmured, and kissed her again before she made herself walk away.

They had lingered so long over the excellent dinner Bonnie prepared the next evening that it was almost dark by the time they decided to take a walk in the garden afterward. Bonnie ducked into the inn first to make sure everything was going well inside, but she felt no need to entertain the guests making use of the public parlor. A few guests were outside enjoying the pleasant weather, but other than a greeting and a friendly nod, they didn't try to converse with Bonnie and Paul.

Though the first of August was still three days away, Paul could tell that the days were beginning to shorten just a bit, the shadows slanting longer, earlier. Summer was winding down. Within a few weeks, his daughter would be married, her other family resettled in Texas, and he would be back in front of his classes, teaching polynomials and differential equations.

Yet he'd be free to do anything he wanted when he wasn't working, he reminded himself quickly. Hang out with the guys, do a little hiking and fishing, kayaking and mountain biking until the season changed, skiing and snowboarding afterward. With the exception of his work obligations, he wouldn't have to check with anyone before making plans, or be back at any certain time. Wouldn't be expected to drop everything if someone needed a ride or a sports coach. He'd experience the carefree bachelor's life he'd never had a chance to live in his youth. It would be fun. Really. Just great.

"Is this the infamous rosebush that attacked your brother?" he asked, nodding toward the unusually variegated blooms that deepened from light pink to deep salmon. This bush sat a little apart from the rest of the garden, in a roomy, cleared niche shaded by a couple of nice trees but otherwise unlandscaped. On the far side of the clearing, a dense stand of woods marked the border of the inn's grounds. A sign sat at the opening of a trail that disappeared into the woods, marking the beginning of the hiking trail that had been pointed out to him on an earlier tour. He had yet to explore it, but he thought he might sometime before the wedding.

Bonnie smiled. "No, that was the big one at the other end of the garden. Kinley, Logan and I planted this one a couple of months ago, on what would have been our mother's birthday. This was her favorite rose, but it's somewhat difficult to track down. We finally found one, and we've all been babying it ever since to keep it alive."

"That's a nice gesture. Keeping her memory with you here in the gardens."

She nodded. "We want to dedicate the meditation garden we plan to install here eventually to the memory of the family members who made this dream possible. Our great-grandparents, who built the place, our mom, who taught us to love it, Aunt Helen and Uncle Leo, who left it for us. We're going to put in a nice koi pond with a little bridge over it leading to the trailhead, a few pieces of nice outdoor sculpture, more flowers and maybe some of those little LED lights that slowly change colors, though Logan's not so sure about that.

We've already bought a couple of nice teak benches we found on sale and that we have in storage until we decide exactly where to place them. I had the idea recently to call it Finley's Nook—Finley was my mother's family name."

"That sounds real nice."

She nodded. "Turns out koi ponds are rather expensive if you do them right. It will be a while before we get to that project because we're putting in some new outside-access restrooms this winter, under the back deck. But we'll get it done eventually."

"I'm sure you will."

"My mother loved koi ponds. When we were growing up in Knoxville, she used to take us to the University of Tennessee to see the water gardens. They were so pretty."

She looked down at the shriveled rose in her hand. Paul laid his hand on her shoulder, thinking of his own tired, sweet mother. "I miss mine, too."

Shaking off her momentary wistfulness, Bonnie met his eyes again. "You said your mother had a chance to see Cassie before she passed away?"

"Yes, she died when Cassie was almost two. Needless to say, my mom adored her grandbaby and spent as much time with her as she could."

Tilting her head, Bonnie searched his face, looking interested in the turn their conversation had taken. "How did she react when you told her?"

"That Holly was pregnant?" He grimaced. "She was upset at first, afraid I'd thrown away my future. But when she saw that Holly and I were both determined to finish school and make a good life for our daughter, she decided to be happy about it."

"And Holly's parents?"

"Yelled at us both, cried a little, then pitched in to help as much as we'd let them. They're nice people. Probably handled it all much better than I would have if it had been Cassie in our predicament," he admitted ruefully.

Bonnie's phone chirped in her pocket to announce a text and she gave an apologetic murmur as she pulled it out to read the message. Knowing that she was always on call here, he wasn't bothered by the interruption.

"Odd," she murmured. "Kinley asked if I was in the inn or at home. Probably has something to ask me and doesn't want to interrupt if I'm busy."

She typed a couple of words into her phone, then held it loosely in one hand as she turned her attention back to him. "I know how your parents reacted when they found out Cassie was on the way. What about you? How did you feel when you found out?"

He thought back more than twenty-one years, trying to come up with words to succinctly sum up the emotions he'd felt. "Stupid. Scared. Unprepared. Guilty. I was afraid I'd ruined my life and Holly's and maybe an innocent child's. I told her I'd marry her immediately and I meant it, but our parents talked us out of doing anything that rash, thank goodness. So I vowed to stand by her and help her in whatever way she needed, but I was still conflicted about it—until they placed Cassie in my arms. As clichéd as it sounds, I knew right then that my life would never be the same. In a good way."

She appeared fascinated by the revelations. "You were so young."

"I guess I grew up fast."

"You missed out on a lot, I think."

"I gained more," he said with a light shrug. "I can play now that my daughter is grown and out of the nest."

Biting her lower lip, Bonnie looked up at him through her lashes, the early evening shadows gathering on her face and masking the expression in her eyes from him. Before she could speak again, they were interrupted by her sister's voice.

"Bonnie! There you are."

Both Paul and Bonnie turned in response to the hail. Kinley rushed toward them along the garden path. She was followed more sedately by Logan, who led a massive black-and-brown dog on a leash—the notorious Ninja, no doubt—and a taller, dark-haired man Paul assumed to be Kinley's boyfriend, whom he'd never met.

Bonnie looked surprised to see the group bearing down on them. "Is something wrong?"

"No," Kinley said with a broad smile that could almost light the darkening garden. "Just the opposite."

"Don't look at me for answers," Logan said with a shrug, his expression quizzical. "Ninja and I were just taking a walk when Kinley ambushed us and insisted we help her find you."

Kinley turned her smile to Paul, who was beginning to suspect what was to come. "I'm sorry to interrupt, but we—well, I couldn't wait. Paul Drennan, this is Dan Phelan."

Paul reached out to shake the other man's hand, receiving a rather apologetic smile of greeting. "Nice to meet you, Dan."

"You, too, Paul. And, uh, sorry to crash your walk with Bonnie."

Kinley shook her head impatiently. "Anyway…"

She held up her left hand, wiggling the ring finger and confirming Paul's prediction. "Dan brought me a souvenir from his trip to New York. I thought you all might like to see it."

Bonnie pounced, grabbing her sister's hand and angling it so that the nearest overhead light made the ring glitter impressively. "You're engaged?"

"We're engaged," Dan confirmed, putting an arm around Kinley's shoulders. "I asked her to marry me, and she said yes."

"Oh, I'm so happy for you both!" Bonnie threw her arms around the taller couple in an enthusiastic group hug.

Though he felt a bit awkward at being included in this private family moment, Paul couldn't help but smile in response to their obvious joy. Even Logan smiled as he kissed Kinley's cheek and clapped Dan's shoulder, visibly approving of the union. Oddly enough, though, Logan's big dog began to make a weird sound that sort of resembled a growl, though his short tail swished the air behind him. Paul took an involuntary step backward, wondering if perhaps the dog was disturbed by the stranger in the midst of the family.

Bonnie noticed his movement, glanced at Ninja, then smiled in sudden understanding. "He isn't growling," she assured him. "That's the sound he makes when he's happy."

"I told you," Logan said, reaching down to give his pet a roughly affectionate ear rub. "He's a weird dog."

When Ninja showed interest in him, Paul extended a careful hand to be sniffed and approved, then patted the dog's back when Ninja wagged and wiggled in an encouraging signal. They took a moment to get to know each other while the Carmichael family continued to celebrate the good news.

"Okay, this calls for toasts," Bonnie asserted, wiping her eyes with the back of one hand. "I have an apple crumble and ice cream for anyone who wants dessert. I can probably find a doggie biscuit for Ninja, too."

She'd offered dessert to Paul after dinner, but they'd decided to take their walk first. He figured now that the private part of their evening was over. Dan gave Paul another contrite look. "Didn't mean to crash your date, Paul," he said quietly as Bonnie herded the others toward her apartment. "We were just excited to share our news."

"I don't blame you at all. Congratulations, Dan, I'm sure you and Kinley will be very happy together."

"Thank you."

"Paul? Dan? Are you guys coming?" Bonnie called over her shoulder.

Paul thought maybe he should go and let the family spend this evening together, but he couldn't leave without saying goodnight to Bonnie and she was already rushing away. He fell into step behind them.

Bonnie headed straight for the kitchen to pull out the sparkling white wine Paul had brought with him that evening. They'd each had a glass with dinner, but still a little more than half remained in the bottle, enough for everyone to make a toast.

Paul motioned toward the door, murmuring to Bonnie, "Maybe I should—"

"Have a toast with us," she said, pressing a flute into his hand. "Kinley enjoys a large audience."

"Why, yes, I do," her sister agreed with a grin and

a toss of her head, making her brown bob swing at her chin. "I've never been shy about taking a bow."

"She's not kidding about that," Logan said, bending to unsnap the leash from Ninja's collar. "Why do you think we've made her the public face of the business? Bonnie and I prefer to do our jobs a bit more...quietly. Kinley likes being out there making presentations and hustling for business and taking credit."

Kinley tilted her head and tapped her chin in a thoughtful gesture. "I'd get mad," she said, then dropped her hand with a smile, "but I'm too happy right now. And besides, you're probably right."

Dan laughed and planted a smacking kiss on Kinley's mouth. "That's why I love her," he said. "I've always admired her brutal honesty."

"Ahem." Bonnie held up her glass and motioned for the others to take theirs. "Perhaps we can stop sniping at each other long enough to get through this toast? Logan, do you want to make it?"

Paul was a little surprised when her brother shrugged and nodded. "Sure. I think I remember the words."

Turning toward the happy couple, he lifted his glass. "To Kinley and Dan. I won't try this in Gaelic, but here goes. May the best you've ever seen, be the worst you'll ever see. May the mouse never leave your pantry with a teardrop in his eye. May you always keep healthy and hearty until you're old enough to die. May you always be just as happy as we wish you now to be."

"Sláinte," Paul added, raising his glass at the conclusion of the translated, traditional Scottish toast. He had to admit he'd been startled to hear it coming from the usually stern lips of habitually gruff Logan Car-

michael, but apparently when it came to his sisters, Logan had a soft side.

Kinley beamed at Paul, then hugged her brother. "Thank you, Logan."

"I'm not saying it in Gaelic for the wedding," he warned her brusquely, though he returned the hug warmly enough. "You know my Gaelic sucks."

"Uncle Leo tried to teach us all some of the Scottish Gaelic he learned from his parents," Bonnie explained to Paul with a little laugh. "He told us our Tennessee accents made it difficult."

Paul remembered Kinley mentioning to Cassie during one of their early consultations that she and Bonnie had hosted a few Gaelic-themed weddings, with bagpipes and kilts and sashes, not such a surprise in this area settled by so many Scots-Irish immigrants. He, too, came from Scottish stock, though as far as he knew none of his more recent ancestors had spoken the language. He knew only a few words that he'd picked up here and there.

"I'm going to head home now," he announced, setting his glass on the counter. "I know you have an early start tomorrow, Bonnie, so thank you for dinner and I'll see you in class tomorrow night. Kinley, Dan—congratulations and much happiness to you both. And it was good to see you again, Logan."

Ninja bumped his leg, making that quirky sound again, tail still wagging. Paul looked down with a laugh. "Yes, Ninja, it was nice to meet you, too."

Bonnie set down her glass hastily. "I'll walk you to your car. Kinley, the dessert is on the counter if you want to serve. I'm sure Dan wants some," she added with a teasing nod at her future brother-in-law, who apparently had a sweet tooth. "I'll be right back."

"Take your time," Kinley replied with a wink.

Chapter Nine

A few minutes later, Bonnie looked up at Paul beside the driver's door of his car. Lights glowed in most of the windows of the inn now, bathing the gardens in amber light, but he didn't see anyone else out and about at the moment. A breeze ruffled the leaves around them, carrying the faint scent of roses with it.

"I didn't expect our evening together to end this way," she said.

"It's a happy occasion for your family. You wouldn't have wanted them to delay telling you."

"Thanks for understanding." She wrinkled her nose and gave a little laugh. "She knew I was seeing you tonight. I think she might have texted me to make sure I was, um, receiving company."

Catching her drift, he chuckled a bit ruefully. "As excited as she was to share her news with you, she must have been relieved to hear we were in the garden and not in your bedroom."

"Hmm." She ran a hand lightly up his arm. "Maybe next time?"

He swooped down to kiss her, letting her have just a glimpse of the frustration he was feeling at that moment. This wasn't how he'd anticipated their evening ending, but he understood. Family came first. Always.

"Will you be at the market in the morning?" she asked with a little sigh that seemed to echo his thoughts.

"I don't think so." As much as he enjoyed spending time with her, he'd rather not have his classmates watch every interaction between them as they were beginning to do. He'd enjoy the final session with the group, but if he had another chance to stroll the market with Bonnie, he'd rather do so without an audience. "I'll be here in time for class, though."

She nodded, and if she was disappointed that he wouldn't be joining them in the morning she didn't let it show. "Good night, Paul."

He kissed her again, taking advantage of their momentary privacy to press her against his car and give them both a taste of what they were missing. Both of them were gasping for oxygen by the time the kiss ended.

Paul had a very uncomfortable drive home. The only thought that made him feel a bit better was the memory of Bonnie saying, "Next time."

Bonnie told herself it wasn't unprofessional for her to hope Paul stayed after class Tuesday night, at which time she planned to invite him down to her apartment for a "conference" with the teacher. She gave him no extra perks during class, she'd charged him the same as everyone else and as she'd pointed out several times, she wasn't giving out grades. Nobody cared if one particular classmate hung around afterward. Even Jennifer had seemed to resignedly accept that for now at least, Paul had eyes only for the teacher.

Last night's dinner date had not at all ended the way she'd envisioned, though she couldn't regret having celebrated with Kinley and Dan and Logan until quite late. Her sister's joy was palpable, and Dan seemed so happy about the future they would build together. Kinley hadn't looked nearly that happy when she'd announced her first engagement to a man she'd married not because she'd been madly in love with him, but because they had seemed like a suitable match. Her heart had not been broken by the failure of that marriage, but her confidence had been badly shaken. Falling in love with Dan and knowing he loved her in return had done wonders for her battered ego.

Bonnie was thrilled for her sister. But tonight, she was glad her family had other things to do, leaving her free to pursue her own pleasures.

She dismissed the class for the final time with a sense of satisfaction that the lessons had gone well. She wasn't sure she wanted to do another multisession class again anytime soon, but she'd enjoyed teaching. Maybe she'd set up more single session classes on next year's calendar. But she would think about that later.

Nora led her classmates in a round of applause after Bonnie thanked them for their participation. "That was a wonderful class, Bonnie," she said as they all began to gather their things. "I'm sorry it's over. I've learned so much."

A chorus of seconds followed the endorsement. Bonnie thanked them repeatedly, promised to send out email announcements about future classes to anyone who'd signed up for notifications and herded them toward the exit. As she had expected—hoped—Paul remained behind.

He started automatically helping her clean up, returning the dining room and kitchen to a state of preparation for the next morning's breakfast service. "It really was a great class, Bonnie."

"Thank you. I worried that I wouldn't be able to hold everyone's attention for six hours of instruction, but it did seem to work out well. I made a few notes about things I can do better in the future, but all in all, I was satisfied."

"You should be." Without being asked, he opened a high cupboard and stashed away a few items he already knew she kept there. "I'm really glad I ran into you at the market that morning so I was able to participate."

Only a month ago, she realized somewhat dazedly. During that time, she'd gotten to see him as so much more than the devoted father of a bride. She knew him now as a teacher, a student, an athlete, a rescuer, a friend and a lover. And there was no aspect of him that she didn't like. Although, *like* didn't seem exactly the right word for her feelings for Paul. Not that this was the right time to analyze her emotions.

"Would you like to come down to my place for coffee or tea?" she asked. "All I have to do first is make a quick check in the parlor to see if anyone needs anything."

"I would love a cup of coffee," he said so quickly that he must have been just waiting for her to ask.

She smiled. “Okay, give me just a few—”

Her phone rang in her pocket, making her jump. Laughing a bit sheepishly, she lifted it to her ear, noting the call came from room five upstairs.

“Bonnie? This is Justine English, in room five. I think you’d better come up here. We have a little problem.”

Thinking she’d be delivering clean towels or finding batteries for a TV remote, Bonnie asked lightly, “What can I do for you, Mrs. English?”

“There’s water coming out from under the bathroom sink. My sister and I have been trying to mop it up but it keeps coming out. We think maybe the pipe broke.”

Bonnie grimaced. “I’m on my way up. Don’t go back in the bathroom, Mrs. English. I don’t want you to slip on a wet floor.”

“Did someone overflow a bathtub?” Paul asked.

She shook her head, already hitting Logan’s number on her phone. “She said a pipe broke and water is running out from under the sink. I have to rush up there to try to stop damage. Logan?” she said as soon as she heard her brother’s voice. “Room five. Water leak.”

“On my way,” her brother said grimly.

“I’m so sorry, Paul.” Bonnie was already dashing into the laundry room for extra towels as she spoke. “I have to deal with this.”

“What can I do to help?”

Moving toward the doorway, she said over her shoulder, “Logan will turn off the water and fix the pipe. I’ll help the two ladies move into a different suite and then clean up the mess. It’s going to take a while. You might as well head home, but thanks for the offer.”

“I’ll call you tomorrow.”

Looking back regretfully, she said, "Please do."

She hated that the evening was ending this way, but she had no other choice, she thought as she dashed for the stairs, assuming Paul would let himself out. He surely understood, but that didn't make her feel any better.

She was tired and grumpy when she changed out of damp, grubby clothes a couple of hours later and donned her pajamas. For the second night in a row, her time with Paul had ended disappointingly. She hadn't even gotten a goodnight kiss this time. The extent of her disappointment was a bit daunting in itself.

She was getting in too deep, she thought, climbing into her lonely bed. And she wasn't talking about the water she'd spent half an hour mopping up in room five.

Her phone rang and even the sight of his name on the screen made her breath catch, her heart beat a little faster. Her hand wasn't quite steady when she put the phone to her ear. "Hi."

"Hi. How's the flood?"

"Contained, thank goodness."

"Any damage?"

She pushed a hand wearily through her hair. "Nothing too bad. Fortunately, the ladies saw the water very quickly. The floor is tiled, so that was okay. The wood underneath the sink will probably have to be replaced, but Logan said that's not too major. We won't even have to turn it in to insurance. He thinks he can have the job completed tomorrow, so I don't think we'll have to lose any of our bookings."

"I'm glad to hear that."

"Yes. If the leak had sprung when the room was empty, it could have been much worse. Logan's going to start checking pipes in all the suites next week, just in case there are any other problems we're unaware of."

"Sounds like a good idea."

"It's an old building. Always something needing attention."

"I'm sure."

She couldn't think of anything more to say about the averted catastrophe at that moment. Instead, she said, "I'm sorry I rushed away from—"

"Don't apologize again," he broke in with an undertone of humor in his voice. "Seriously, Bonnie, I get it. You have big responsibilities there. I'm not going to get in your way."

She frowned. She was glad he wasn't annoyed at being brushed off by her two nights in a row, but did he have to be quite so sanguine about it? He could at least sound a little disappointed.

"So, do you have any big plans for the rest of the week?" she asked, groping for an innocuous conversational topic.

"Cassie and I have decided to take our bikes out tomorrow. She had some plans that fell through, so we're going to ride the Creeper Trail one more time before she leaves."

"All thirty-five miles?" A multipurpose trail formed from an old railroad line, the Virginia Creeper Trail ran from Abingdon, Virginia, to Whitetop, Virginia, near the North Carolina state line. Winding through national forest and crossing old restored trestles that offered spectacular views, the trail was a popular local attraction for guests of the inn, some of whom brought their own mountain bikes, others who rented bikes from outfitters or preferred taking hikes along the trail.

"That's the plan. We're packing picnics and figuring to take six hours or so to complete the ride. Already made arrangements for a shuttle service. Have you ever ridden the Creeper Trail?"

"I've made the ride from Whitetop Station to Damascus." That seventeen-mile section of the trail was mostly downhill, steeply so at times, and a favorite with tourists. "It was beautiful. I had a great time."

"I wish you could go with us tomorrow. Damascus to Abingdon is a great ride, too."

"Maybe I'll get a chance to do the whole trail soon."

"I'd be happy to ride with you anytime."

"Sounds great," she said brightly, though she wondered how long it would be before they could make good on that offer. And whether he would still be interested in taking her by the time she was free to go.

"Speaking of Cassie, she told me your dress is almost ready. I think she's going to call you tomorrow evening to set up a time to deliver it to you and take your picture in it for her portfolio."

"I can't wait to see it. I'll definitely make time for her." Bonnie wasn't sure if Cassie could wait until her shower on Sunday to take the photos for her class, but surely there would be a half hour or so beforehand when they could take care of it. "Tell her to call me anytime."

"I'll pass along the message."

"Have fun on your ride with her tomorrow," she said, hearing a hint of wistfulness in her own voice. "It's nice that you can enjoy another father-daughter adventure before she moves away."

"Did your dad ever take you on bike rides?"

"Not that I remember. Dad's what some people call

a foodie. He always treated us to the most exotic restaurant he could find while he was in town to have us sample foods that were out of our usual experience. He complained about what he called a lack of true variety in the Knoxville area, but really there were quite a few interesting international food choices. And he almost always took us to Dollywood in Pigeon Forge when he was in Tennessee, usually once every summer, though sometimes he was gone more than a year at a time. He's a big Dolly Parton fan," she added with a slightly hollow laugh.

She didn't hear an answering smile in Paul's voice. "When was the last time you saw him?"

"He was here the weekend we reopened to guests. That will be two years ago in November, so it's been a year and eight months or so. I talked to him fairly recently by phone, though, and he sends email updates and photos from his travels. He's been exploring Australia and New Zealand since he left here."

"If you don't mind my asking, how does he support himself when he's globe-trotting?"

"He has a couple of import and export partners here in the States. Dad makes overseas connections and they handle U.S. distribution. I've never asked a lot of questions, frankly, but he seems to get by okay. I know he sent money to our mother regularly when we were growing up. All of us refused to accept any more from him after we turned eighteen, though we encouraged him to stay in touch with us. We attended college on scholarships and work programs, but we felt uncomfortable taking money from him when he'd never been that much a part of our lives."

"It had to have been tough for you and Kinley and

Logan, growing up without your dad in your life," he said a bit tentatively. "For the most part, I mean."

"Harder for Logan, I think. I was so young when he left that I can't say I pined for him, exactly, since I didn't really remember him being there full time. But yeah, I missed having a full-time dad in my life. I was never surprised, but always disappointed when he left after his visits. I'd have loved to have been as close to him as you are with Cassie. You've done a wonderful job staying involved with her even though you weren't married to her mom."

"I'm sorry you didn't have a better relationship with your father."

"It's certainly not at all the kind of relationship I'd want for my own children and their father," she admitted, then added firmly, "But we had a great childhood. We adored our mom, and we had our great-uncle Leo, who was like a dad to her and a grandfather for us. We had busy social lives in Knoxville, and I had my big brother to watch out for me—a responsibility he always took very seriously."

Paul cleared his throat. "Yeah, I might have noticed that."

She laughed. "He's not really so scary. He just likes to growl—sort of like his dog."

He paused a moment, then said, "I guess I should let you get some rest. I'm sure you have an early start planned for tomorrow."

"The usual," she admitted. "I'm glad you called. I really hated having to rush away from you the way I did."

"I know. And as much as I understood, I regretted it, too." His deep tone gave her a hint of the way he'd have preferred the evening to end, instead. Which would not have included her sitting in her bed alone at the moment, she thought with a swallowed sigh.

"Would you be free to join me for dinner Thursday evening?" she asked hopefully. "We'll have a full inn and there's an event scheduled, so I can't go far in case anything comes up, but we could eat at Bride Mountain Café, or I could cook. I mean, I have to eat, right?"

Perhaps it wasn't the most graceful invitation, but he didn't seem to mind. "I'd like that. I'll even treat at the café so you don't have to cook."

"Why don't we meet here at six-thirty, then? We can leave your car here and walk down to the café." And she would insist on treating, since it had been her idea, but she saw no reason to argue with him about that just now.

"Sounds good."

"Good night, Paul."

"Sleep well, Bonnie."

As if she could, she thought, setting her phone on the nightstand and hoping there were no more frantic calls that night. Something told her she would be thinking about Paul long into the wee hours.

After all her blithe promises to her siblings—and to herself—that she would be cautious, would guard her heart and not invest too much too soon, she was very much afraid she was foolishly falling in love with Paul. She might well have done so the first time she'd collided with him, and had felt a spark jolt between them when he'd helped her up. Yet even after spending these lovely days with him since, even after the most intense, most spectacular lovemaking she'd ever experienced in her life, she still wasn't sure exactly what they were doing together.

Did he truly see her as a summer dalliance, a way of entertaining himself during this break from school, like his kayaking and soccer playing and horseback and mountain bike rides? Was he perhaps subconsciously using her to fill his emptiness at the thought of his daughter and her other family leaving him behind? Did he really like her, with an eye toward a possible future? How was a woman supposed to know what a man was thinking without just coming right out and asking? Or was he counting the days until he could take off for China or North Dakota or some beach somewhere? Their discussion about her father had reminded her of all the reasons she had tried so hard to be careful.

She punched her pillow in frustration. Kinley would probably have no trouble being so bluntly candid; Logan certainly wouldn't. But she wasn't sure she was quite as confident as her sister and brother when it came to relationships. Going toe-to-toe with her siblings was very different than setting herself up for heartbreak with a man whose mere touch could make her world spin.

Paul arrived at the inn Thursday evening to find it a hive of frantic activity. People mingled on the front porch and a huge white tent was set up on the east-side lawn. Everyone seemed to be dressed in business casual style. It didn't look like a wedding, he mused. Even as he drove into the front parking lot, he was assailed by the barbecue scents wafting from several large portable grills. Men in white aprons and chefs' hats were flipping what looked to be steaks and burgers while lines of eager diners lined up to be served. He could even see a bar at one side of the tent, with servers pouring wine and beer.

Because the parking lot was full, he drove around back to park beside Bonnie, figuring she wouldn't mind since she'd directed him there before. He was a little early, so he thought she might still be upstairs. Just in case, he tapped on her apartment door, but when there was no answer, he moved toward the deck stairs, pulling out his phone in case he needed to text her that he had arrived. Recorded jazz music drifted to him from the party, not overly loud but easy enough to hear from this side of the grounds. He stepped onto the large deck at the same time as Logan, who'd climbed the steps on the opposite side. They exchanged nods of greeting.

Paul motioned in the direction of the tent, though that side of the inn wasn't visible from where they stood at the big back doors that led into the dining room. "What's going on?"

Logan shrugged. "Some sort of charity fundraiser thing Kinley booked. They have their own people to set up, cater and clear away, so we didn't have to do anything for this one except provide the grounds."

He moved quickly aside when two women hurried out from inside the inn, nearly bumping into him as they rushed toward the party with murmurs of apology. Paul noticed that Logan moved quite agilely despite his slight limp.

Logan spoke wryly. "Sure will be glad when we get those outside-entrance bathrooms installed. It'll be a little more trouble for the cleaning staff, but better in the long run than having people running in and out these doors."

"The rooms will be beneath this deck, right?"

Logan nodded. "Two doors, one for men, one for women, each leading into a small lounge area with attached toilet facilities. No showers or anything like that, but wedding parties can change clothes and other people can use the amenities. I mean, they'll still be welcome to go inside the inn, if they'd prefer, but the extra conveniences will really come in handy."

It was the longest conversation he'd ever had with Bonnie's brother and they were talking about bathrooms, Paul thought with sudden wry amusement. "Were you going inside?"

Logan nodded and led the way into the dining room. Paul saw that the round tables were covered with white linens and decorated with fresh flower centerpieces, but not otherwise set up for food service, making him assume nothing was scheduled in here until breakfast tomorrow morning.

"Guess you're here to see Bonnie?"

"Yes, we're having dinner."

Logan looked as though there was something he wanted to say, but whatever it was, he kept it to himself. Remembering Bonnie's comment about her brother being overprotective, Paul thought it was probably just as well Logan had swallowed the words. Saying he had to change a lightbulb in one of the rooms upstairs, Logan moved on, leaving Paul with a quizzical smile.

He had thought he might find Bonnie in the kitchen, but the immaculate room was empty. She could be upstairs, he thought, or maybe in the office behind the reception desk or in the front parlor with guests. He decided to check the parlor and then text her that she could find him there when she was ready. It seemed as good a place to wait as any.

He stopped abruptly in the arched doorway to the parlor. This room had been set up for old-fashioned, unplugged social entertainment with couches and chairs arranged for conversation, two game tables at one end of the room, and a tall bookcase filled with board games. Another beautiful chandelier hung from the tall ceiling, and the bay window was covered with lace. Bonnie stood in that window, looking absolutely radiant in the late-day light streaming in from outside as she modeled cheerfully for Cassie, who was fidgeting with a digital camera nearby. Kinley sat on one of the sofas, laughing and offering suggestions for poses.

Paul was aware of Kinley and his daughter, but he couldn't seem to tear his gaze from Bonnie. She looked…stunning. Young, sexy, vibrant. The bright green dress set off her golden hair, vivid blue eyes and flawless fair complexion. And what it did for her figure…

He swallowed. Hugging her curves, the dress had tiny cap sleeves and a deep, square neckline that made the most of her cleavage. It pinched in below her bust with a band that made her waist look even tinier than he knew it to be. When she turned as instructed to present the back for Cassie's camera, he saw that the garment closed at her nape with a decorative button, beneath which a large, triangular cut-out revealed a creamy swath of bare back down to the sewn-in waistband. The dress ended with a sassy little pleat at the back of her knees.

For the first time since he'd met her, he saw her in heels. Strappy gold sandals did amazing things to her legs that he'd always admired anyway. Mugging for the camera, having not yet noticed him in the doorway, she lifted one leg behind her and tossed back her head in a playful, pinup girl pose that sent a wave of hot blood straight to his groin. He pushed his hands casually into his pockets and drew a few deep breaths, glad he was no longer a callow youth who couldn't control his body—though he had to admit, it was a close call for a few minutes there. Damn, she looked good.

Suddenly seeming to sense him there, she looked toward the doorway and quickly straightened, her cheeks going a little pink. "Oh. Hi."

"Hi," he said gravely, leaning against the doorjamb. "Am I interrupting?"

"You're early."

"A little. Hello, Kinley. And, Cassie, you didn't tell me you'd be here this afternoon."

Looking down at her camera screen, Cassie answered distractedly. "It was sort of last-minute. Bonnie said she could take a few minutes if I came right now. Bonnie, these are great. Exactly what I need for my portfolio. Thank you so much."

"Are you kidding? I can't believe I'm getting this beautiful dress just for doing a few fittings for you."

"It is a gorgeous dress," Kinley said, almost enviously. "If it wasn't five inches too short for me, I'd steal it in a heartbeat. I can't wait to see your collections in the stores someday soon, Cassie."

Cassie, of course, was thrilled by the praise. She beamed. "I hope so. London is such an exciting place to study design."

"I'm sure you're going to have a wonderful time."

"I think so, too. I can't wait to be there with Mike. I've missed him so much."

Paul managed not to sigh, though he had to admit his daughter's obvious impatience to move away made him want to.

"I'm sure you have missed him," Kinley said sympathetically. "My fiancé travels quite a bit, too, though at least he's usually in the same country as I am. He's hoping to travel less once we're married and do more freelance work from our house here."

"You're engaged?" Cassie looked up eagerly from stashing her camera in its case. "I hadn't heard."

"It's very recent. This week, actually. Your dad happened to be here when we made the announcement."

"You didn't tell me, Dad." Cassie shot a look of reproof at him, then pounced on Kinley. "Let's see the ring."

Bonnie moved toward Paul. "It will take me just a few minutes to change for dinner," she promised. "This dress is a little fancy for the café."

"You look beautiful in it," he said simply.

"Thank you. Cassie did a great job with it, didn't she? She's very talented."

"When are you getting married?" Cassie asked Kinley, who had stood to display her ring.

"We're talking about a winter wedding. That's our slower time here at the inn, so it would be best for me."

"I know you'll both be very happy." Cassie gave Kinley an impulsive hug, sharing their mutual joy.

All this marriage talk was making Paul a bit uncomfortable. Avoiding Bonnie's eyes, he told himself it was because he didn't like the reminder of how quickly his daughter's wedding was approaching.

To be honest, he'd been feeling a little antsy ever since Bonnie had made that passing remark on the phone last night about what she would want in a father for her own children. It had reminded him of a similar incident a couple of weeks earlier when she joked about having her kitchen step stool in her wedding. Taken together, did those comments mean she was less "married" to her job than Nora had jokingly implied, perhaps hearing the faint ticking of a biological clock? Was she influenced by being surrounded by weddings all the time, by her own sister's engagement? Or was he merely projecting emotions on to her she wasn't feeling at all?

As far as he knew, she had just been thinking out loud about the future when she was ready to settle down and start a family, and he was just someone with whom to enjoy her rare time off from work in the meantime. She'd given no indication that she wanted more. From him, at least.

"So, tell me, Kinley. Did you see the ghost bride?"

Bonnie stumbled slightly on one high heel when Cassie asked the question. Paul reached out quickly to steady her.

"I, um—" Kinley gave a funny little laugh. "That's just a romantic old legend, Cassie. I don't need to see a ghost to tell me that Dan and I are going to have a long, happy marriage."

Cassie sighed deeply. "Still, it would be cool to see her, wouldn't it?"

"Your dad and I are going to walk down to the café for dinner," Bonnie announced quickly. "Maybe you'd like to join us?"

Cassie glanced at Paul in question. It was obvious

that she'd like to join them, but wasn't entirely sure he wanted her to. "You wouldn't mind, Dad?"

"Why would I mind?" he asked with a chuckle. "It's a public restaurant. And your table manners haven't embarrassed me in public since you stopped blowing bubbles through your drinking straws."

She giggled. "Mom stopped that quickly enough. Okay, I'd love to have dinner with you. We can tell Bonnie all about our ride yesterday. I have tons of pictures on my phone if you want to see them, Bonnie. It was so beautiful."

"I would love to see them," she said and Paul was impressed that she even sounded sincere about it.

"Are you coming with us, Kinley?" Cassie asked.

Kinley shook her head with a smile. "Thanks, but I'll hang around here until the charity fundraiser is over, just in case they need me for anything. The organizer is a friend of mine and we gave her a reduced rate for the grounds rental, so she's bringing in a couple of steak dinners for Logan and me."

"Steak sounds good to me," Logan said from behind Paul, who moved out of the doorway to let him enter. "Bonnie, I changed that bulb in the hallway. That was all tonight, wasn't it?"

"That's all. Paul, Cassie, I'll meet you on the front porch in five minutes," Bonnie promised, already heading out, the high heels altering her usual brisk walk. Logan and Kinley followed her out, heading for the kitchen.

"I feel kind of bad about crashing your date," Cassie said as she and Paul moved into the foyer. "You're sure you don't mind?"

"Sweetheart, I'm delighted." He put an arm around

her and gave her a smacking kiss on the cheek. "I want to have as many dinners with you as I can get in the next few weeks."

She nestled into his shoulder. "Thank you, Daddy."

"But after dessert, you can disappear," he added, making her giggle.

"Yes, Daddy."

Chapter Ten

True to her word, Bonnie rejoined them in only a little over five minutes, a little winded and pink-cheeked from hurrying, but still looking very pretty in her more typical top, skirt and flats. They walked down the wide, paved road together to the Bride Mountain Café. The road dead-ended at the inn, so there wasn't a lot of traffic most days, Bonnie explained, but the café did a good business from her guests, tourists and locals alike. On the outside the diner was plain, though bright green canopies provided an air of welcome. Inside, though, the décor was more inviting—simple, clean and bright—with delicious aromas that made Paul realize just how hungry he was.

Once they were seated by a slender brunette who greeted Bonnie familiarly, then introduced herself to Paul and Cassie as the owner, Liz Miller, they all ordered the dinner special—chicken and dumplings with bacon-seasoned green beans, a small side salad and cornbread which Bonnie assured them was "to die for."

Cassie made sure there were no awkward silences during the lively meal. Not that Paul and Bonnie had ever had trouble talking anyway. Cassie showed off the photos on her phone and chattered about the bike ride, and of course the subject then turned back to her wedding festivities, starting with the wedding shower the coming Sunday.

"I've had nothing to do with it," she said with a laugh. "My maid of honor—my friend Noelle, who has been my bestie since high school—she's taking care of everything."

Bonnie nodded, having met Noelle several times while making arrangements for the shower. "Noelle knows exactly what she wants for the shower. She's given me very specific directions about the hors d'oeuvres I'm preparing and serving to the guests. She's been very pleasant about it," she added quickly when Cassie gave a little wince. "It's actually easier for me to have clear instructions about what the clients want."

"I have instructions, too," Paul said with a chuckle. "Noelle informed me I'm to show up at the end of the shower and help Cassie transport the gifts to my house so she can get them packaged and shipped off to London."

Cassie rolled her eyes comically. "I told everyone they didn't have to bother with gifts, but you know how friends can be..."

"They want to give you things for your new home,"

Bonnie said. "It's only natural that your friends would want to do that."

"Don't worry, honey, we'll get everything packed and shipped," Paul assured his daughter. "Your mom and I will help you with it."

"I know. Just so much to do."

"And you like it that way," he teased her, making her dimple and admit that he was probably right.

They indulged in peach cobbler after the meal, though Cassie and Bonnie shared an order. Paul wanted his own dessert. With ice cream. He laughingly assured them he had calories to spare, thanks to yesterday's bike ride.

When they'd finished, they walked back to the inn where the fundraiser was winding down, most of the guests beginning to pile into cars. Cassie almost immediately announced that she had to go, giving her dad a wink as she spoke. "Thanks for dinner, Dad. And, Bonnie, I enjoyed seeing you. I'll see you again Sunday, okay?"

Paul stood back and watched as his daughter and Bonnie exchanged quick cheek kisses. "Thank you again for the dress, Cassie. It's so beautiful. I know you'll get full credit from your class."

Cassie laughed and turned toward her car. "I have no doubt."

"There's that modesty again," Paul muttered loud enough for his daughter to hear even as she hurried away, so that she left them with a laugh.

Paul turned back to Bonnie, who was looking up at him with a smile that didn't quite seem to reach her eyes. "Tea?" she offered.

"I'd like that."

She nodded. “Let’s go through the inn to the back so I can make sure everything is okay.”

“Of course.”

Fifteen minutes later she closed her apartment door behind them, pushing a hand through her hair in a slightly weary gesture. Seeing that, he reached out to lightly squeeze her shoulder. “Tired?”

She dropped her hand. “A little. Crazy week.”

“Why don’t you sit and I’ll make tea for us both?” She kept her kettle on the stove, and he’d seen her take tea bags from a wooden box on the counter, so he thought he could handle that.

Smiling up at him, she placed her hands on his chest. “Actually, I don’t really want tea.”

He slipped his arms around her, his heart starting to thud against his chest. “Neither do I,” he confessed. “But if you’re too tired...”

Laughing softly, she tugged his head down to hers. “I think I can find just enough energy for this.”

The kiss was explosive, heated by all the pent-up frustration of the past few days. He held her tightly against him, and she crowded even closer as if it still wasn’t enough for her. It certainly wasn’t enough for him.

She gave a little push against his chest, and he dropped his arms immediately, thinking maybe she was too tired, after all. Instead, she gave him a slow smile and took his hand. Without a word, she turned and moved toward her bedroom.

Articles of clothing fell just inside the bedroom door, at the foot of the bed, next to the head of the bed. They lowered themselves to the bedclothes, snuggled together and slowed down to savor with long, tender kisses and soothing strokes. Bonnie's little purrs were music to Paul's ears, letting him know she took pleasure in his touch, that their caresses were as arousing to her as they were to him.

"Mmm," she murmured, when he rubbed his hand in slow circles on her back, gently massaging the knots he found there. "This is exactly what I needed tonight."

What she needed tonight, he repeated to himself. No mention of the future, no reason to think she was reading anything more into this than she should. A few hours of pleasure. He couldn't help wondering how many more nights he would have with her. How many more times they could be together this way, so easily. So passionately. He was beginning to wonder if he would ever be able to walk away from her without leaving a part of his heart behind—and that was a fear he'd never really faced with anyone else.

"Paul?" Bonnie caught his face between her hands and drew back enough to give him a quizzical glance. "You look so stern all of a sudden. Is everything okay?"

What the hell was he doing? He was in bed with a beautiful, willing woman and he was wasting time trying to predict their future?

He rolled her beneath him, pressing her into the pillows with his best imitation of a pirate's grin. "Most definitely okay."

Reaching up, she wrapped her arms around his neck and drew his mouth down to hers. "Good," she murmured against his lips. And then, a moment later, "*Very* good."

The wedding shower for Cassie on Sunday afternoon was a big success, and the food Bonnie served received glowing reviews. She hadn't wanted to be too heavy-handed with Cassie's wedding colors of pistachio, dove-gray and coral, but she'd incorporated all of the colors in the antipasto and petit four trays, in tiny sandwiches and canapés and, of course, little bowls of pistachios and mints. She didn't make the stunningly beautiful cake, which was purchased from a bakery in Christiansburg, but it looked exactly right amidst her own contributions.

There weren't a lot of guests, only Cassie's closest friends, her sister and mother, but it was a cheery group with a lot of laughter, chatter and genuine happiness for Cassie. Bonnie stayed quietly in the background for the most part, keeping an eye on the food, discreetly refilling coffee carafes and water pitchers. Cassie opened gifts with squeals of appreciation. Then, almost before Bonnie knew it, the guests began to leave.

Which meant that Paul should be arriving soon, she thought with a thrill of anticipation.

She hadn't seen him since he'd left her apartment late Thursday night, though they'd spoken by phone Friday and Saturday nights. There'd just been no time to get together. Their chats had been light and easy. They'd talked of her work and his preparations for the coming new school year, of the wedding preparations and funny things the twins had said. They did not talk about the future, nor about any feelings they might have for each other. Any time the conversation had strayed too close to either of those subjects, they'd both quickly deflected it. She certainly didn't want to admit her deepening feelings for him over the phone, or discuss her concerns about whether she meant more to him than a friend with benefits—very nice benefits, but increasingly not enough for her.

One of the shower guests paused in front of Bonnie, a tiny baby in her arms. Bonnie hadn't even heard the infant fuss during the event, though she'd seen her passed around and cooed over quite a bit. "This is such a beautiful place," the woman said. "I can see why Cassie decided to have her wedding here. I'm Lynn, by the way."

"Thank you, Lynn. We're delighted Cassie chose us. I've been admiring your baby during the shower. She's been so good," she said, leaning in to get a better look at the sweet little face beneath a stretchy pink lace headband adorned with a white lace rosette. "What's her name?"

"Alanna. She's five weeks old. My husband had to work unexpectedly today and I couldn't bear to miss the shower, so Noelle said I should just bring her with me."

Alanna's eyes were open, trained on Bonnie's face with that puzzled, intrigued, slightly unfocused look unique to infants. "Is she always this quiet?"

"Most of the time. But when she gets wound up, she can pretty much bust your eardrums. Would you like to hold her while I get my things and say goodbye to Cassie?"

Bonnie blinked a little in surprise, since she didn't even know the woman—but her hands were practically itching to get ahold of this tiny vision in pink-and-white lace. "I would love to."

The transfer went smoothly. Lynn stepped away to gather her things and speak with her friends, though Bonnie noticed she kept a close eye on the baby, understandably so. Alanna seemed perfectly content to be held by a stranger, looking wide-eyed at the room around them, her gaze occasionally locking on Bonnie's face. Bonnie was quite sure she wore a sappy smile as she cooed at the infant, and when she was rewarded with a quick, toothless smile, she laughed delightedly.

"You," she crooned, "are an angel. Just about the cutest baby ever."

Alanna made a sweet little sound accompanied by a funny face that caused Bonnie to laugh again. When it came to babies, she was just such a girl, she thought wryly.

She'd been so focused on the baby that she didn't immediately notice Paul had arrived. She glanced up just in time to see him staring at her with a startled expression before Lynn came to reclaim her child. All the guests departed, leaving Bonnie with Cassie, her mother and sister. And her father.

"Dad, look at all the nice gifts my friends gave me," Cassie urged him, motioning toward the items displayed on a table. "Wasn't that sweet of them? I'm going to miss them all so much."

Paul pointed a finger at his daughter, speaking in a stern voice underlaid with a note of humor. "Don't even start that. I've gotten enough tears from your sister."

Fourteen-year-old Jenna, a cute brunette with braces on her teeth and a hint of freckles across her short nose, put her hands on her hips and shook her head. "I didn't cry, Uncle Paul. All my friends did," she insisted.

"Uh-huh."

In response to his teasing skepticism, she rolled her

eyes in a way only teenagers could pull off so eloquently.

While Bonnie began to tackle her part of the cleanup, Cassie and her family repacked gifts and carried them out to the parking lot. Bonnie couldn't help watching Paul interacting with his daughter's mother and half sister. He was so easy and comfortable with them, his affection for them visible on his face. His behavior toward Holly wasn't exactly fraternal, but very close to it. Considering they'd known each other since childhood and had been platonic partners in child-raising for more than twenty years, Bonnie supposed that made sense.

With everything packed away, Holly reminded Jenna that they had plans for the evening. She took her leave of Bonnie graciously—the way she seemed to do everything, Bonnie couldn't help thinking. "I'm sure we'll see each other several times during the next couple of weeks," Holly said. "We're getting down to the wire."

"Be sure and let us know if there's anything at all you and Cassie need from us."

Holly smiled and pressed Bonnie's hand. "We will, thank you. Come on, Jenna, let's go."

Bonnie watched through her lashes as Paul brushed a kiss against Holly's cheek, then gave Jenna a hug and a head tousle.

"Don't forget you promised to take Jackson and me to the movie Wednesday," the girl reminded him.

"I won't forget. I'm bringing my headphones and an audio book," he assured her gravely, earning himself another eye-roll.

"The movie won't be that bad," she said. "You might even like it if you'd just give it a chance."

"A film about a bunch of teenagers acting out and making fun of adults? Honey, I'll be seeing that every day in just a few weeks. Not my idea of comedy."

Jenna was laughing as her mother escorted her out. "You're just counting the days till you're free from all of us and don't have to haul us around," she said over her shoulder.

"Hooray for freedom," he quipped, his smile revealing little of his thoughts, though Bonnie searched his face carefully. Was Jenna right?

Cassie dashed out soon afterward, stopping to hug her dad and Bonnie on the way to the door. "Best shower ever," she assured Bonnie fervently.

The inn seemed unusually quiet after Cassie left. Bonnie heard a few footsteps upstairs, and a couple of muted voices drifting from the parlor. She had almost two hours before the guests assembled for the Sunday evening sandwiches.

"Do you have to rush off?" she asked Paul.

He shook his head. He was still smiling, but something about his eyes looked different to her. Darker, perhaps, not quite reflecting his smile. "I can stay a little longer."

Perhaps he was just tired, or a little melancholy from Jenna's reminder of the big changes coming in his life. "Would you like to take a walk in the garden? I wouldn't mind some fresh air."

He nodded. "That sounds good."

He opened the back door for her, then stood back so she could go out first. A wave of humid heat engulfed her when she stepped out. August had begun with a vengeance, as if to make up for the unseasonably cool and rainy month just past. A bee buzzed past her and she heard the drone of a weed trimmer around the side of the inn, proving that Logan wasn't letting the heat keep him from his work. She hoped he would remember to stay hydrated, then told herself to stop worrying. Her brother could take care of himself; it was simply old habit for her to fret about his health after the serious illness that had felled him in college. The long-gone tumor in his leg had left him with a slight limp, a determination to stay fit and healthy, and a few trust issues when it came to anyone outside his family, but he didn't need her hovering over him all these years later.

The fountain splashed invitingly, but she saw that another couple was already standing beside it, enjoying the fine, cool mist that hung in the air. The couple had checked in earlier that day, explaining that the woman was attending a three-day conference at Virginia Tech and that they had chosen to stay at the inn rather than at a hotel in town so her husband could take advantage of nearby hiking trails while she networked with business associates. Though they seemed nice enough, Bonnie angled away from them, figuring she would visit with them over sandwiches later.

Paul walked quietly beside her toward the back of the garden where the koi pond would be someday. He seemed to be lost in his thoughts, and she wasn't quite sure how to draw him out as she was somewhat preoccupied with her own.

She looked up at him, moistening her lips. "Paul—"

He looked beyond her with a frown, toward the hiking path that disappeared into the woods. "What was that?"

She turned just in time to see a flash of white dissolve into the foliage. "I missed it. What did it look like to you?"

"For a minute I thought someone was watching us, but I guess I was wrong."

"I'll bet it was a white-tailed deer. We do have a lot of them up here. Logan wages a constant battle to keep them from destroying his landscaping."

"Yeah, that's probably what I saw." With one last glance toward the trail, Paul turned back toward her. "You were going to say something?"

She pushed her hands into her skirt pockets, toying with her phone, that ever-present reminder of her responsibilities here. "Cassie had a nice shower, didn't she? She has some very nice friends."

It was clear that he could tell the inane comment hadn't been what she had initially intended to say. He frowned at her for a moment, then shrugged and nodded. "Yeah, she's always been lucky to have a good group of friends."

"They seemed like an energetic crowd. I'm sure they've had some fun times together."

"Oh, yeah." He cleared his throat, his smile looking forced. "You looked right at home among them when I arrived. Made me remember that you're not much older than Cassie and her friends."

Bonnie wrinkled her nose, wondering if that was what had been bothering him during their walk. "I'm sure from Jenna's perspective, anyone over twenty is ancient," she said, hoping to keep the age thing in perspective. "Just a number, right?"

"No." He reached up to squeeze the back of his neck, his expression impossible to read. "It's more than a number. It's a stage of life. And you and I—well, we're at different stages. Hell, I could be a grandfather in the not-so-distant future."

Logan had pointed out that same possibility. Her eyes narrowing, Bonnie responded now the same way she had with her brother. "And that matters why?"

"Just putting it out there. The point is, you're insanely busy here at the inn, and I figure you'd be better off spending your free time with someone closer to your own age, someone at the same place in life where you are. You know, someone who's ready to settle down, ready to start fresh with babies and diapers and preschool and all that other stuff I dealt with years ago and that you haven't had a chance to experience yet."

Her hands clenched in her pockets. She could feel her spine stiffening with each word he said. "You think that's best for me, do you?"

He nodded, continuing doggedly. "With Cassie's wedding coming up in a couple of weeks, and school starting back a couple of weeks after that, it's a hectic time for all of us. Once I'm back at work, I won't have weekdays off like I do now, and your weekends are booked, so finding time to hang out could be difficult. We said we were just having fun for the summer, and I have. I've had a great time. I hope you've enjoyed our time together, too. And I hope we can remain friends."

"Friends," she repeated coolly. "Like you are with the other women you've dated. Holly and Tim's sister, and probably a few others."

"Well, yeah..." He eyed her warily, seeming to sense something in her attitude he couldn't quite interpret. Still, he continued determinedly, almost as if he were reciting, "It's better to end things on friendly terms. We'll be left with very pleasant memories. I care about you quite a lot, Bonnie, and I hope you'll smile when you remember the time we spent together, the adventures we crammed into a relatively short time. Maybe we can have coffee or something sometime."

He motioned vaguely with one hand. "So, anyway, maybe this wasn't the ideal time to have this discussion—I mean, I know you still have a lot to do this evening, but I thought it best for me to make sure I haven't been leading you on, or keeping you from meeting someone closer to your age."

"Well, isn't that oh-so-noble of you?"

Paul blinked in response to her tone, making her realize he'd never seen her lose her temper. He was very, very close to finding out just what an experience that could be.

"I'm not implying that you *were* expecting anything from me," he assured her quickly. "You're the one who said you weren't looking for strings, and I'm not conceited enough to imply that I consider myself an irresistible catch. Like I said, I just thought it best for me to make sure you know that I'm not looking to follow my daughter down the aisle."

She wasn't sure she'd ever been so angry in her entire life. Maybe pain was fueling her temper, but at the moment she was too mad to acknowledge even to herself how badly he had just hurt her. True, she'd wanted to have a serious discussion with him, and she'd been prepared that she might not hear what she hoped from him—but this had not been a dialogue. It had been a condescending monologue that had infuriated her.

She drew a deep, ragged breath and spoke with icy

precision. "I can't tell you how grateful I am to you for looking out for my best interests. You know, being so much older and wiser than I am, of course."

He grimaced. "Uh, Bonnie—"

"Let me just make something clear to *you*, Paul," she said over him. "We will not be friends from this point, though I will be extremely polite and professional during your daughter's wedding festivities. My friends—and I do have a few, despite my busy work life—give me credit for knowing what's best for myself without their guidance. They have intelligent, adult discussions with me rather than making unilateral decisions that affect me. And they *ask* me what I want, rather than tell me what I should want!"

"Look, I—"

"I swear to God, Paul, you'd better leave now," she advised him through gritted teeth. "If you say one more condescending word, I might just be tempted to punch you right in the face, if I could reach it."

"I can reach him." With his dog at his side, Logan emerged from the hiking trail just in time to hear the latter part of her threat. Logan glared at Paul while Ninja looked in bewilderment from one tense human to another. "Do I need to punch him, Bon?"

She whirled on her brother and poked him in the chest with one finger. "No. If I need to punch someone, I'll handle it myself—even if I have to find a stepladder to do so."

Logan nodded, not looking at all surprised. "Yeah, you would. Just letting you know you've got backup, if you need it."

So grateful for her brother's endorsement of her self-sufficiency that she'd have thrown her arms around him if Paul hadn't still been standing there, she tossed her head and glanced over her shoulder at Paul.

"Please tell your daughter to let us know if there's anything at all we can do for her during the next two weeks," she said with the exceedingly courteous professionalism she had so furiously promised him. "Assure her that the staff of Bride Mountain Inn will do everything in our power to make sure her wedding day is everything she wants it to be. I trust you won't think it 'best' for her to change her venue at this late date?"

"Of course not," he said impatiently, looking more than a little irritated himself. "Bonnie—"

"I have to take care of my guests now. I'll see you at the rehearsal, I'm sure. Goodbye, Paul."

He looked frankly stunned as he stared at her for a moment. It was very obvious that this conversation had not gone as he had planned, that she had not reacted the way he'd expected. Had he thought there would be tears? Gratitude that he had so gallantly spared her from future disappointment? He'd been very wrong.

Without another word, he turned and walked away. He didn't look back.

Logan waited until Paul was out of sight before speaking again. "I didn't catch what set that off, but if you need to talk…"

Any other time, the reluctant sincerity in his offer might have amused her. As it was, she merely shook her head. "I'll be okay, but thank you."

"You know where to find me."

She nodded. She would find him here, at their inn, just as he would find her there if he needed her. Later, when she lay in bed, undoubtedly sleepless and in angry pain, she would comfort herself with the knowledge that though her father in her childhood and the first man she'd loved as an adult might have walked away, her brother and sister and the inn would always be there for her. All in all, she supposed she was actually lucky. She was simply having trouble believing that at the moment.

Chapter Eleven

Something had gone very wrong. And Paul was painfully aware that it had all been his fault.

It had taken him more than a week to reach that brilliant conclusion. Over and over, he had mentally replayed the words he'd said to Bonnie in the garden. He'd made versions of that same speech several times before, and had been on the receiving end a few times, and while those previous encounters had occasionally been awkward, they had usually ended amicably. To be honest, the women with whom he'd previously agreed to be no more than friends had looked somewhat relieved rather than disappointed—an ego hit for him, but undeniably best in the long run. Merely more confirmation that he just wasn't the settle-down-for-life type. Not from choice, exactly—more by nature, he supposed. It just never seemed to work out.

He'd tried to make Bonnie understand that. He'd used all the key phrases that had seemed to work before. *I hope we can remain friends... I've enjoyed our time together... I hope your memories of me make you smile... I care about you.*

Maybe we can have coffee together sometime, he thought with a groan, dropping his head onto his kitchen table.

"Dad?" Cassie paused in the doorway on the way out of the house. She and Mike, who was staying with his parents until the wedding, were having dinner with her other family that Wednesday evening, then staying late to watch movies with her half brother and sister. This would be the last night before her wedding when they'd be free to hang out with the twins. "Is something wrong?"

He straightened immediately. "No. Just tired. You have fun tonight, okay?"

"Are you sure you won't come with me? You know they'd love to have you join us all for dinner one last time."

One last time. The words made his chest clench, though he managed a smile. "Don't be so dramatic, Cassie, there will be family dinners in the future. We'll all get together in Dallas next time you and Mike are in the States."

She took a step closer to the table, her eyes a bit damp. "I don't like seeing you unhappy."

"I'm not unhappy," he said—lied—firmly. "I'm going to miss you. I'll miss all of you. But I'll be fine. I've already signed up for a new rugby team some of my friends are getting together. I haven't played rugby in a decade and I'll probably break a hip but it'll be—"

"Daddy." Her hand fell gently on his shoulder. "Why don't you try talking to her? If you'd just—"

Now it was his turn to cut in. "We've already discussed this, Cassie. We're not going to talk about Bonnie."

All he had told his daughter was that he and Bonnie were no longer seeing each other socially. As far as Cassie knew, Bonnie was the one who'd made that choice, and Paul was content to leave it at that. The thing was, though Cassie had seen him part ways with lady friends in the past, she had never known him to genuinely hurt after those partings. Apparently his uncannily astute daughter could see that he was hurting like hell now.

Cassie exhaled gustily. "Fine. Just let her go without even trying. End up alone. Is that what you want?"

He leveled a chiding look at her. "You're telling me I should get involved with someone just to keep myself from being lonely after you leave? That would be rather selfish of me, don't you think?"

"Yes, it would," she replied evenly. "If that was really the reason. But that isn't why you were seeing Bonnie, was it, Dad? I think you genuinely cared for her, and it had nothing to do with me getting married or Mom and Larry and the kids moving away."

"Go have dinner, Cassie. I love you, but this is really none of your business."

She didn't take offense, but leaned over to kiss his cheek. "I know. And I love you, too. So talk to her, okay, Dad?"

He remained silent, and she left with a little sigh of resignation. It wouldn't be the last he'd hear of it, he figured, but he would remain adamant about not discussing it.

For one thing, he had a feeling that if he told his daughter exactly what he'd said to Bonnie, Cassie would lose her temper with him, too.

My friends give me credit for knowing what's best for myself without their guidance. They have intelligent, adult discussions with me rather than making unilateral decisions that affect me. And they ask me what I want, rather than tell me what I should want!

He could still hear Bonnie's words almost as clearly as if she stood in front of him saying them again. And yet it had taken him over a week to really hear what she had said, to process and understand the words.

He hadn't asked her what she wanted. He'd simply broken it off with her without warning, and with his lofty—and, as she'd said, condescending—excuses that he didn't want to keep her from finding someone who would offer her marriage and children and all those other things he thought she should want.

He had been an idiot. An arrogant jackass. She'd have had every right to climb on a stepladder and punch him in the face.

Yet the worst part about it, he thought as he buried his face in his hands, was that he still wasn't entirely certain he'd been wrong.

"You know you don't have to go out there," Kinley told Bonnie with a look of sympathy as they stood in the inn's kitchen early Friday evening. "Dan and Logan and I can handle everything tonight. We can say you aren't feeling well."

Bonnie drew herself up to her full five feet, three

inches, her chin held high. "You'll do no such thing. I have a job to do and I will perform it very well, thank you."

Kinley glanced at Dan with a rueful smile, and Bonnie saw him shake his head in what appeared to be bemused admiration. "Way to tell her, Bonnie," he murmured.

Cassie's wedding rehearsal would be starting soon. The inn's suites were filled with out-of-town guests, and members of the wedding party were already arriving for the rehearsal. Bonnie had already seen and spoken to Cassie and Holly, but she hadn't yet crossed paths with Paul. That was the ordeal Kinley was trying to spare her by offering this excuse.

Kinley didn't know what, exactly, had gone wrong between Bonnie and Paul, but Bonnie had told her that it hadn't been a pleasant parting. She had at the same time assured her sister that the breakup would not in any way affect her work for Cassie's wedding.

In their meetings Bonnie had seen Cassie all but biting her tongue to keep from blurting out comments or questions about what had happened between her dad and Bonnie, but she'd managed to hold them back. Bonnie assumed Paul had laid down very strict orders to his daughter to stay out of this.

Bonnie would be just as pleasant to Paul as she had been to the others, she promised herself. She didn't consider herself a particularly skilled actor, but she was determined that no outside observer would have a clue from her behavior that she and Paul were anything more than innkeeper and client. They would not be friends. And from now on, she swore, she would never again get involved with a client or guest. The way she'd hurt for the past twelve days, she wasn't sure she would ever get involved with anyone again, though she wanted to believe she hadn't let him shake her quite that badly.

She was still so angry with him that her hands wanted to clench every time he crossed her mind—which, admittedly, was often. She didn't try to let go of that anger. She suspected it was the only thing keeping her from curling into a ball and sobbing.

She could no longer boast that she'd never had her heart broken. Paul had pretty much stomped on it. The worst part was that he'd ambushed her to do so, giving her no chance to prepare herself. At least she hadn't cried in front of him. She had the satisfaction of vowing to herself that she never would.

She picked up a tray of tiny cakes covered in pistachio-green icing, each decorated with a piped *W* for Woodrow, the surname of Cassie's fiancé and the name Cassie had chosen to adopt after the wedding. The cakes and pistachio-and-white-chocolate-chip cookies would be available on the back deck during the rehearsal, along with coffee, iced tea and bottles of water. Dinner would follow at an Italian restaurant ten miles away, where Mike had taken Cassie for their first date.

The wedding would begin at five tomorrow afternoon with dinner on the lawn afterward, served by caterers hired for the occasion.

To Logan's satisfaction, Cassie hadn't asked for elaborate decorations on the grounds. The event would be fairly simple but elegant, with white columns to hold baskets of pale green-and-white orchids, white folding chairs for the guests with each aisle marked at the end by knots of flowers and dove-gray ribbon, discreetly placed fairy lights and garlands of orchids and ribbon for the arch of the gazebo in which she and Mike would take their vows. The musicians would provide their own instruments and sound system, and the officiate would not stand behind a stand or podium, so setup for this wedding had been easier than most.

Tomorrow, the caterer would take care of putting up the tent with hanging chandeliers and tables with white tablecloths and pistachio-and-gray linens and decor. It was going to be a beautiful wedding and Bonnie, for one, would do nothing to dim the celebration.

It was inevitable, of course, that her path would cross Paul that evening. Apparently now was the time. She suspected he made a point to get it over with, approaching her as she set out a fresh tray of cookies just before the start of the rehearsal. He'd probably wanted to be the one in control of this meeting, too, she thought irritably, so he wouldn't be the one caught unprepared if he turned a corner and found her there.

She gave him a glittering smile. "Hello, Paul."

He searched her face with dark, unsmiling eyes. "Bonnie. Everything looks very nice."

Aware that they were being not-so-discreetly watched by the very few people who knew they'd gone out a few times, she kept her smile firmly in place as she said, "Thank you. I believe the rehearsal is about to start. If you'll excuse me, I'll refill the coffee carafes."

He made a quick, almost instinctive move to detain her. "Bonnie—"

Her eyebrow rose in a cool expression. "Yes?"

He paused, then shook his head and sighed. "Never mind."

Nodding, she sidestepped him and headed inside.

She wouldn't cry, she wouldn't cry, she wouldn't cry. The mantra swirled through her head as she busied herself indoors, and it helped her hold off the film of threatening tears. But still her eyes burned even as her heart radiated with pain.

Logan was in the kitchen, pouring himself a cup of coffee when she carried in an empty cookie tray. He took one look at her face and scowled. "You're sure you won't let me pound him? I'd catch him in a hidden nook so none of our other guests would see."

Laughing softly, Bonnie leaned her head against her brother's arm for a moment. "Thanks for the offer, but no."

"Damn."

She put her hostess smile back on and picked up a full coffee carafe to take outside, leaving her brother muttering unhappily behind her.

She was on the deck when Cassie's wedding planner called out for Paul to practice walking Cassie up the aisle. Though tomorrow they would exit from the dining room doors and cross the deck to the steps down, tonight they waited at the foot of the stairs for the signal. Bonnie couldn't resist watching as the father and daughter negotiated the gravel path to the gazebo where the happy young groom waited. At the foot of the steps to the gazebo, Paul tenderly kissed Cassie's cheek. Bonnie suspected plenty of eyes filled with tears at that moment, though her own remained stubbornly dry. Had she not been so angry, she'd have probably sobbed buckets.

Standing at Bonnie's side, Kinley sighed. "You think Dad will be in the country for my wedding?"

"He said he'd try, didn't he? Maybe he will." Bonnie

tried to speak with her usual optimism but she found that a bit more difficult these days.

Given the signal that his role was completed, Paul turned away from the gazebo. Maybe it was just a coincidence that he looked up at the deck, that his eyes met hers at that moment. It took all the strength she had to make herself turn away.

It was late, she was tired, and she knew she needed to get some sleep that night, but she couldn't turn off her mind. She tossed and turned in the bed for a while, then paced the apartment, finally settling on the couch with the TV remote in her hand. And then she stared at the dark screen of the television, having no interest in turning it on.

When someone tapped on her door, she thought it must be Logan. He'd probably been doing one of his midnight prowls and had seen her lights on. She sighed, figuring she'd have to reassure him again that she was fine. Maybe if she told him enough, she'd start to believe it herself.

The sight of Paul standing at her door made her heart stop beating. At least, that was the way it felt when she finally started to breathe again. "What are you doing here?"

His expression was impossible to read in the dim security lighting. "I saw the lights in your windows."

"You just happened to be driving by?" It was a sarcastic question, of course. The rehearsal had ended hours ago, as she was sure the dinner afterward had. And of course there was nowhere to drive except to the inn on the dead-end road up Bride Mountain.

"Actually, I drove a couple of our guests back after

the dinner," he said, providing at least a partially credible explanation. He blew that by adding, "That was more than an hour ago."

Tightening the thin robe she wore over her pajamas, she asked, "And what have you been doing since?"

"I sat in my car in the parking lot for a while. Started driving down the hill and got as far as the café. Sat in my car in the parking lot there, too."

She'd wrapped the ends of her robe belt around her hands so fiercely her fingers ached, but she didn't loosen it. "Why are you here?"

"I need to talk to you. May I come in? Or we could talk in the garden if you'd be more comfortable outside."

Their last talk in the garden hadn't gone well. But she wasn't so sure she wanted to invite him in, either. Not if it was only so he could kick her heart around some more.

After hesitating for several long moments, she sighed sharply and moved out of the doorway. "Fine. Come in and say what you have to say. But if you're here to convince me that we need to be coffee buddies, you're wasting your breath."

He winced and closed the door slowly behind him. "I'm so sorry I hurt you."

"You did hurt me," she agreed honestly. "But mostly, you made me furious."

"Yeah, I got that idea."

He offered a tentative smile that she didn't return. His faded quickly. "I've thought very hard about what you said. I was arrogant."

"Yes." She had no intention of making this easy for

him, though her heart was beating so fast now she was almost afraid he could hear it.

"I was condescending."

"Yes."

"I was terrified."

Having been prepared to agree with whatever derogatory adjective he'd come up with next, she blinked. "Why?"

Squeezing the back of his neck, he sighed, looking so weary and sad that she almost reached out to him instinctively. She curled her fingers in her belt again to stop herself. "Because," he said, "I walked into the inn and saw you holding a baby. And it knocked the socks off me."

"See, that's what I meant by arrogant," she said, her temper igniting again. "You just assumed I was angling for you to marry me and make babies with me. Maybe I was hoping something might happen between us, maybe I wasn't, but the least you could have done was talk with me about what I wanted, how I felt. About what you wanted, or didn't want. Making an arbitrary decision to end things between us because you assumed I want marriage and kids was way overstepping your bounds. I mean, if you were tired of me, if you were no longer interested in seeing me that way, fine. Say so. I'd get over it. But don't give me that obnoxiously noble song and dance about doing it for my sake, and all because you aren't prepared to give me what you're so sure I want or need."

"Bonnie—"

She was on a roll. "I don't know exactly what I want for the future yet, okay? I mean, I've always vaguely envisioned having kids someday, but I don't know.

Maybe if you and I had grown closer and we'd talked about it, I'd have decided I could be happy without kids, like Uncle Leo and Aunt Helen were. Maybe I'll have that talk with someone else someday. But you needn't panic just because you saw me holding a baby. I won't interfere with all this great new freedom you'll have after tomorrow."

"Actually, you totally misunderstood the cause for my panic," he said quietly. "It wasn't because I was picturing you holding a child of mine. It's because I had a sudden vision of you holding a baby you'd had with someone else."

"I— What?"

He dropped the hand he'd been using to massage his neck, letting his arms hang loosely at his sides. "You just looked so young and fresh and pretty standing there. And there was my daughter, opening wedding gifts and being teased about having babies soon—and I pictured you meeting someone else, someone younger and with a less complicated history, and I could almost hear you giving me the speech about always being friends, so I thought maybe I should just save you the trouble. It's the way all my relationships have ended, so I've just started expecting it. I've even told myself I liked it that way."

He shrugged. "Like you said, I made a prediction of what was going to happen between us, but it wasn't the one you thought. It wasn't even the one I expected, to be honest. But I suppose it was still arrogant. I came to apologize for hurting you—for making you angry," he corrected himself. "Maybe it's too late for us to be friends now, and maybe there was never a real chance that it could have been anything more, but at the very least I didn't want it to end with a fight."

Bonnie was so confused now her head was spinning. She pushed her hands into her hair in an effort to stop it. "Are you saying you *didn't* want to stop seeing me?"

"Of course I don't want to stop seeing you. I just—well, I don't want it to be all fun and games between us anymore, knowing that any day you could pull out the let's-just-be-friends talk. Trust me, this is as much of a surprise to me as I'm sure it is to you, but I've discovered that I want more than that this time."

She dropped her hands and studied his face intently. "And you wouldn't necessarily rule out maybe getting married someday? Or maybe even having another child?"

She could almost hear him swallow. "I, uh, I'd be open to the possibility. If it was what you wanted. What we both wanted," he added hastily, maybe afraid she would take that wrong, again. "As I've told you, I've loved being a dad. Maybe—well, maybe it's something I wouldn't mind so much doing again."

Her heart was beating so hard, so fast. Did he know what he was saying? Could she really trust him to mean it this time?

"And all this freedom you're coming into? Your first chance since you were just a kid to do whatever you want, whenever you want?"

She thought she saw the first glimmer of a smile in his eyes. "And if what I want is to be with you, whenever we get the chance…?"

She gave him a wistful little smile in return, her shaky resistance to him shattering. "Let's just say I'm open to the possibility."

He took a step toward her. “Bonnie?”

She rested her hands on his chest, the tension easing slowly from her clenched muscles. “I’m still kind of mad at you.”

He cupped her face in one hand, his expression soft with regret. “I know. And I’ll do whatever I can to make it up to you.”

“I was really angry,” she warned, her hands sliding up and around his neck. “Making up could take a while.”

“Whatever it takes,” he promised, his lips moving lightly against hers. “Have I mentioned that I’ve fallen in love with you, Bonnie Carmichael?”

Her breath caught in her throat. “Okay, you just made a lot of progress in making up. I love you, too, Paul Drennan.”

She felt tears pressing at the back of her eyes, but she melted into his embrace without letting them fall. They didn’t have much more time to be together on this glorious night. She wasn’t going to waste a minute of it with tears.

The wedding was as beautiful as any bride could have wished. Cassie glowed in the stunning white dress she had designed and sewn for herself, a long, fitted sheath with the tiny cap sleeves she seemed to favor, a deeply draped back and a clever little train that draped into a V from midcalf. Her maid of honor wore pearl gray, and the two bridesmaids, one of whom was her half-sister Jenna, were in pistachio green. An adorable little toddler served as flower girl, her dress pistachio with a silvery sash tied into a big bow at the back and the ring bearer wore a tiny gray tux. The groom and his attendants wore pale gray suits with white shirts and pistachio ties. The flowers carried out the colors with pale gray ribbons, green orchids and accents of coral roses. The weather cooperated, warm but not horribly so, the sky clear and a light breeze to fan cheeks and ruffle hair.

Because Cassie had wanted them there, Bonnie and Kinley were guests at the wedding as well as official hosts. They sat in folding chairs at the back of the bride's side, Bonnie in the green dress Cassie had made for her, Kinley in one of her stylish summer suits. Paul had asked Bonnie if she wanted to sit at the front with him, but she'd declined, saying she thought it was a little soon for that step. She thoroughly enjoyed the wedding, watching as Cassie and Mike said their vows so confidently and contentedly in front of their friends and family.

Afterward, there was much celebration around the food tables beneath the lawn tent. Cassie really did have a large support group, Bonnie mused, watching as Cassie's mother, stepfather, siblings, maternal grandparents, a few aunts, uncles, cousins and dozens of friends mingled, ate and chattered.

An arm went around her waist from behind and she gazed up with a smile at Paul, who looked so handsome in his gray suit and tie. "It was one of the most beautiful weddings I've ever seen," she said sincerely. "And trust me, I've seen a few weddings in my time."

He smiled, and she was pleased to see that the gleam had returned to his jade eyes. "I thought it was nice, too. But I missed having you sitting beside me."

"Maybe at the next wedding we attend," she said lightly.

He lifted her left hand to his lips, placing a sweet kiss against the ring finger. "Or maybe you'll be standing beside me at the next wedding we attend," he murmured.

She looked up at him with widened eyes. "That sounded almost like a proposal."

Whatever panic he'd felt only a few days before seemed to have melted away with the expressions of love last night, and the intimately heated hours that had followed. His grin was broad and bright when he looked at her in challenge and said, "And if it was?"

Her heart swelling in her chest, she leaned against him, resting her head against his heart. "Let's just say I'm open to the possibility."

She and Paul were finally able to be alone together in her bedroom several hours later. The wedding guests had departed, except for the few that remained in suites upstairs. Amid tears and smiles and hails of good wishes, the newly married Cassie and Mike had taken their leave to begin their new life together. Some of the wedding decorations had already been taken down and stashed away, and Logan and his crew would take care of the rest tomorrow. Bonnie had the rest of the night free, until the morning when she would start all over again with her brunch preparations.

She was happy.

With the bedroom lamp dimmed cozily behind her, she moved to the window to draw the drapes. She paused for a moment with her hand on the draw-pull, looking out over the gardens. She was at ground level, looking out straight into the flowers and foliage at the path that led to the meditation garden. As she stood there, fog drifted in ribbons across that dark path barely lit by the discreetly placed security lighting and the bright late summer moon. The scene looked almost magical.

Paul stepped up behind her, wrapping his arms around her waist and looking out over her head. "Looks very peaceful. I can see why you love living here so much."

"Yes. It never gets old for me."

As they stood there, a sliver of mist separated, swirled, coalesced into a shimmering column. For only a moment, Bonnie would have sworn she saw a pale face in that mist, smiling sweetly back at her. She blinked, and the illusion cleared, leaving only the fog dancing across the flowers.

Paul had gone very still. "Did you just see—"

"What?" Bonnie whispered, her skin tingling.

"Never mind." Placing his hand on hers, he drew the curtain, closing them into the privacy of her room. Putting all other thoughts from her mind for now, Bonnie turned into his arms and lifted her face for his kiss. She had all the magic she needed right here.

* * * * *